HOW NOT TO
VAMPIRE

SEASON 1

a vampire uninstruction novel by

RODNEY V. SMITH

L ST
bajan
B O O K S

First Edition: September 2021
Published 2021, by Lost Bajan Publishing
www.lostbajanbooks.com
North York, ON M2J 2C6, Canada

Interior design by Rodney V. Smith
Cover Photograph by Theik Smith
Edited by Debra Goelz

ISBN: 978-1775007289
ISBN-13: 978-1775007289

10 9 8 7 6 5 4 3 2 1

Dedication

To Allison, my wife and inspiration, who laughs at my bad jokes.

To Deb for constantly kicking my ass into gear and only laughing at all of the good jokes.

HOW NOT TO VAMPIRE

SEASON 1:

SO I MIGHT BE A VAMPIRE

Pro-Tip for Humans #146:
If you think your life sucks, try mine sometime.

Chapter 1
MY OWN WORST ENEMY

You know that dream you have where some unknown assailant grabs you by the legs and drags you forcefully from your bed, only for you to smash your head on the floor and force you to wake the fuck up?

Me either.

So for that actual thing to happen to me was a hell of a shock.

My day began with an explosion of agony in the back of my skull. It wasn't the usual type that was preceded by a night of heavy partying when someone else was paying the bill. No, this was a different type of pain completely. It was the type that would have rendered a person unconscious, but it kind of gets complicated when that person is *already* unconscious. So instead of getting knocked the fuck out, I was essentially knocked the fuck awake, pain spiking through my head, my ears ringing in a kind of *you just got a concussion* way.

Just to add to the insult and confusion, there was something over my head. Through the pain and fog that had become my brain, I realized that I should be freaking the fuck out. I couldn't see what was going on, but I could feel hands on both my legs and *holy shit I was being dragged across the floor!*

"Wait," I mumbled instead of yelling something utterly heroic and incomprehensible. In situations like this, what exactly is the appropriate thing to yell? Your choices usually come down to a variation of *"Hey, stop doing that, hey you, stop,"* or a lot of wordless yelling.

The dragging suddenly stopped. I didn't even have time to wonder what that meant before somebody punched me in the face, one, two, three times, adding to my ongoing head trauma.

"Ow," I managed, and then whatever was on my head was ripped away.

I slowly blinked at the two very pissed-off women who stared down at me, my brain trying and failing to connect the faces with names. I was also desperately trying not to think about how I was only wearing my Superman skivvies and that I had suddenly become a line from a Weezer song. Finally, something clicked--

"Tanya! Doreen!" I blustered as cheerfully as I could, which wasn't much to be honest. The pain that was masquerading as my brain had come with the conclusion that this might all be a stupid prank. "You had me worried for a second there. I thought it was somebody who *actually* wanted to kill me."

"Hi Bob," Doreen smiled nervously. "Nice underwear," she said, blushing. Doreen looked tough, the sides of her head shaved with the remaining hair at the top dyed blue and pulled back into a ponytail, but that was by design. Doreen had always been a sweetheart to me, and I was honestly surprised she had been roped into this mess, whatever it was. At least she was a little embarrassed by the sight of all my exposed brown skin. My naked chest probably did nothing for her since she was into chicks, but I was glad that my irregular workout routine had yielded some kind of muscle, and I wasn't too scrawny-looking for my attackers.

I'd like to say that any other female assailants who were not lesbians would have at least been distracted by my manly looks, but who am I kidding? I'm an average height black-Mexican guy (my dad is from Barbados, my mom from Mexico), reasonably good-looking if I don't let my scruff get too long. I'm not a hunka-hunka-burning man-meat, if that's what you're into, but my past girlfriends have always said that I had a particular mischievous look that made them weak in the knees. Since it's hard to get that kind of a reaction in the middle of an assault, I was fucked, especially since one of said assailants (Tanya) had never really liked me.

"We're going to kill you if you don't tell us where they are," Tanya snarled.

See what I mean?

Tanya was short and mean and worked out a lot, but you could tell she skipped leg day at the gym, with those spindly legs of hers and was all about the upper body. She was covered in tattoos, but only had one professionally-done on her left shoulder. She made a point of wearing shirts that displayed it well; it was of a giant eagle on a Canadian flag and was literally labelled "Pride and Joy" just to sell the cliche. The rest had been home-jobs, each exhibiting varying degrees of skill from bad to what-the-fuck.

"Can I call a timeout so we can start over, and you guys can tell me what the fuck it is that you want instead of playing the pronoun game?"

"Hit him again!" Tanya snarled. Doreen looked really apologetic, but she went ahead and punched me again, hard. My head rocked back and collided with the fake wood floor.

"Please stop hitting me!" I groaned, clutching my still unbroken nose. The back of my skull was in agony too, but I couldn't decide which part of it needed the most attention since my brain was now throbbing.

"Sorry," Doreen whispered and then looked embarrassed when Tanya glared at her.

"Tell us where the drugs are, Bob!" Tanya snapped at me.

A moment of clarity struck me. I looked from Doreen to Tanya and then back again, but there was no help from either of them. My brain had finally decided that this wasn't a prank after all, and was now filling my body with a mixture of endorphins and adrenaline.

A panicked thought managed to break through, and I wracked my brain trying to remember if Jaime had spent the night or not. From the amount of light coming through the crack of the curtains in the living room, it looked to be around midday, so even if she had spent the night, she had already left for work, so there was no danger to her, right?

Right. One less thing to freak out about. Now about the other thing—

"Oh come on, you guys. Those aren't my drugs," I protested. "Those are *Julio's* drugs. I'm just holding onto them for him, and you know what? I don't even know if they *are* actually drugs so--"

"Cut the shit, and tell us where they are, dickwad." Tanya growled. She reached into the back of her waistband and pulled out a nasty-looking handgun. From the way she held it, I could tell she knew what she was doing and not just posing. "Are you going to make me ask you again?"

Doreen mouthed something to me that looked like "Just tell her," but it was hard to be sure.

The toilet flushed at that moment and we all froze while we each decided how to react to the sound, at the same time coming to terms with what the flush meant: *there was someone else in the house.*

"Who the fuck is that?" Tanya snarled. She motioned frantically to Doreen, who scurried over to the bathroom door and planted herself against the wall, lying in wait.

"JAIME! STAY IN THERE!" I yelled, and Tanya casually punched me in the nose.

Goddamit!

My yelling had been pointless. The bathroom door clicked and swung open after a moment. Jaime, my girlfriend and love of my life half-danced into the living room, her head lowered as she looked at something in her hands. All we saw of her was a mass of jet black curls that defied the best brushes and any attempts to tame them. There was a white cord running from the curls to the phone in her hands, a definite sign that she was listening to her ongoing collection of favorite songs that I affectionately called *"Jaime's Infinite Playlist."*

She had no idea what was going on.

Jaime looked up and first saw me on the floor, then her eyes went to Tanya, and then they went to Tanya's big fucking gun, which was pointed *right* at Jaime's fucking face.

"Oh for fuck's sake, Bob!" Jaime said.

"Bitch--" Tanya never got to finish what she was going to say. It might have been something along the lines of *"Bitch, you better sit your ass down before I shoot you in the face,"* or something equally charming. Jaime didn't give her the chance to finish. What Tanya and a lot of people didn't know was that my girlfriend kicks ass and the last thing you want to do is to stick a gun in her face.

Jaime had done a stint in the army, long before she met me, and she had absolutely loved it. We always joked about how she could beat me easily with her hands tied behind her back. I was the one in the relationship with zero fighting skills. Jaime on the other hand--

Let's just say that she was fast. Tanya didn't even begin to react as Jaime leaned out of the path of the gun, stepped forward, grabbed Tanya's gun-hand and in a fluid motion, ripped the gun away in the most painful manner possible, almost breaking Tanya's fingers and possibly taking some skin in the process.

"Fuck!" Tanya yelled in pain, pulling her injured hand away.

Jaime stepped back, bringing the gun to bear on Tanya. Or at least she tried to.

Two things happened at once: I scrambled backward, trying to get to my feet, but Tanya stumbled into me and we fell down in a tumble of limbs, and Doreen snuck up from behind Jaime and clapped her hands together hard with Jaime's head in the middle, in a classic ear-clap. Jaime cried out, dropping the gun, her face twisted in agony,

Of course, Tanya chose that exact moment to sucker punch me, and I reeled backward, my head ringing not quite unlike a bell.

A moment later I was back to kneeling on the floor next to Jaime, a visibly pissed-off Tanya stalking back and forth with the gun in her uninjured hand. Doreen stood behind us, possibly to make sure that Jaime didn't try anything. I snuck a look at Jaime, and she just looked stunned; there was a trickle of blood coming from one ear.

"Okay, we're going back to basics Bobby, you feel me?" Tanya said. "Either you tell me where the drugs are, or I'm going to shoot your bitch in the face."

Pro Tip for Humans #7:
the Secret lives of friends should remain secret.

Chapter 2
A FRIEND IN LOW PLACES

S o there I was, dragged out of bed by two drug dealers and a gun shoved in my face while my girlfriend was threatened with death, just to top things off nicely. Must be a Tuesday.

The love of my life and possibly very-soon-to-be-ex-girlfriend Jaime turned to look at me, at Tanya's death threat, her face twisted with rage and disgust.

There are only so many things you can say in a situation like this and none of them are good. When someone is threatening to kill your girlfriend unless you give up the drugs that you're hiding in your apartment, don't be a dick.

I tried to reason with Tanya. "How about you guys just let Jaime go, and I'll get you anything you want?"

Tanya was far from being reasonable. "Give us the drugs."

"Julio will murder me," I pleaded, looking between her and Doreen. Surely one of them had to see how stupid this whole thing was.

Tanya scoffed. "Sounds like a 'you problem' to me, cuz *I'm* going to murder you." She cocked the gun dramatically. "Drugs now."

I glanced at my pissed off girlfriend and tried one more time. "Let her go and I'll tell you where they are."

"I'm going to put a bullet in her face at the count of three," Tanya helpfully pointed out. "One..."

"Cupboard above the fridge," I muttered, not daring to look at Jaime tis time. "There's a false back. Just give it a nudge."

"Keep an eye on them, sweetie," Tanya said to Doreen, and backed away into the kitchen. She found the step-ladder next to the fridge and quickly set it up to rummage through the cupboard.

"Drugs Bob?" Jaime hissed at me. "*Fucking drugs?*"

"I can explain--"

"Can you really? Because two women in the apartment with guns looking for drugs is really fucking hard to *explain*."

"You're absolutely right," I admitted. "This I can't explain."

I glanced over my shoulder at the well-muscled Doreen and she tried to glower at me but she really wasn't very good at it.

"Psst! Doreen!" I hissed. "Give us a break here will ya?"

Doreen shook her head. I realized after a moment that Jaime was glaring at me.

"You *know* each other?" Jaime asked dumbfounded.

Doreen waved and smiled awkwardly. "You must be Jaime," she said, "Bob talks about you all the time. I'd shake your hand, but you know: working! And besides you might punch me."

I wanted to sink into the floor under the strength of Jaime's laser glare. I thought I had seen her mad before but this was on another level, like I was fucking dead no matter what happened kind of level.

"Tanya and Doreen run drugs for Julio," I mumbled.

That one caught Jaime by surprise.

"Wait, *Julio*? From upstairs? He's a *drug dealer*?"

"It's always the quiet ones," I observed. "You never see it coming."

Tanya climbed down from the ladder, holding the four plastic-wrapped bricks of heroin that Julio had left in my care about a week ago. Each block had been clearly labelled in black Sharpie "JULIO'S HEROIN," to prevent any confusion. I had pointed out to him that it implicated the shit out of him if I got caught with them. He had, in turn, pointed out to me that he was going to murder me if I got caught, so I had more incentive to stay out of trouble.

Julio mostly sold some primo weed, better than the legal marijuana they were selling these days. Every now and again, Julio would come into something a little extra. The last place he wanted to keep his stash was where people would look, so he had a couple of guys on his payroll. It paid well enough, and he always provided a little taste of the product, and that suited me just fine. It was a simple arrangement: as long as we didn't touch the actual product, Julio wouldn't kill us. I had no problems with that. It wasn't like I was a junkie or anything, just your average recreational heroin addict. And yes, such a thing existed: I was living proof of it. *Dammit.*

"We got them," Doreen said in disbelief from behind us. "Can we go now?" Doreen brushed past us to go over to Tanya and took the bricks from her, doing a mini-celebratory dance of joy.

"I hate to break up the party but Julio is going to lose his shit when he finds out about this," I pointed out helpfully. I could see a painful future waiting for me and wasn't liking it, not one bit.

"I'm already losing *my* shit, but don't mind me, I'm just the girlfriend," Jaime murmured from next to me. "That's heroin! In our apartment!"

"That is no heroin--" I bluffed badly.

"Then why the fuck does it have 'Julio's Heroin" written on the side?"

"Okay, you caught me. It's heroin."

"Goddamit, Bob," Jaime hissed.

I tried to ignore her. Maybe I could at least appeal to Tanya's better side. "Guys! Julio doesn't like it when his people fuck with his supply."

Tanya bent down in front of me and put the barrel of her gun under my chin. I met her gaze steadily and tried not to tremble. She had a stupid teardrop tattoo at the corner of her right eye that was very distracting. I wondered if I should tell her and then decided not to.

"You tell Julio a word of this," Tanya threatened, "and I will come back for you. I will kill you and your pretty little girlfriend just to make a point."

"Have you actually met Julio?" I asked in great confusion. "The man is a psychopath. I'm not going to have a choice."

"I'll fucking kill you right now--"

"I don't think so," came a man's voice through the broken front door.

Tanya bolted to her feet and pointed the gun at the man. Doreen spun, fumbling the bricks of heroin and almost dropping them. I was just glad the weapon was out of my face. Sure it was now pointed at Claude but he had more experience with guns.

"Who the fuck are you supposed to be?" Tanya snarled.

"Is that *Claude?*" Jaime hissed, having recognized the voice.

"You can call me Smith," Claude drawled as he sauntered into the kitchen. "It's not my real name of course, but the *right* people know who I am."

It was undeniable that Claude's presence filled the room. It may have had something to do with the black knee-length topcoat that made him look like he had just stepped out of a gangster movie with very well-dressed gangsters, or it might have just been Claude himself. He was a hell of a lot more confident than any man had a right to be when he had a gun pointed at his head by a pissed-off drug dealer. At six-feet two-inches, Claude was taller than I was, and yes, dammit: he was handsome in the way that made women either want to find out all about his dirtiest secrets or give him some new ones. He was what I described as a big damn hero, and in all of the twenty years that I had known him, he had never let me down once. When Claude was around, I was instantly the sidekick, and I didn't mind one bit.

Claude carried a brown McDonald's bag that no doubt contained the breakfast sandwiches he usually brought with him when he dropped by.

"Who the *fuck* are you?" Tanya yelled, and Claude just raised his eyebrow. He made eye contact with me and winked, completely ignoring Tanya, just to send a message that she was no longer in charge, gun or not.

"You okay there, Bob? Jaime?" Claude asked.

I waved and glanced at Jaime who was shaking her head and rolling her eyes.

"Not good at all. I just got my ass kicked... and I think I just got dumped," I grumbled.

"Oh you are *so* dumped," Jaime agreed, glaring daggers at me.

"Well it *is* a Tuesday," Claude reminded me. Tuesdays always sucked for me. I should have just stayed in bed--

"Mister, I'm going to shoot you in the face--" Tanya threatened, waving the gun for emphasis and reminding me that she was the reason I *wasn't* still in bed. Doreen was frozen, eyes darting from Claude to Tanya and back again. I almost felt sorry for her. Almost.

"You really don't want to point that gun at me," Claude advised cooly. He smoothly produced a simple white card in his hand. It was like watching a magic trick. One minute his hand was empty and then, the card was there as if it always had been. "Take it. Everything you need to know is right there."

Doreen inched forward and snatched the card as if Claude might bite. Her face lost all colour as she read it, and she literally began shaking.

"What's the matter with you?" Tanya asked, still keeping her eyes on Claude.

"Leave the drugs," Doreen said softly but forcefully. She gave the card to the curious Tanya, who read the card and nodded in agreement.

Tanya put the gun away. "We're leaving the drugs."

As the broken door valiantly tried to swing shut behind the women, it felt as if all air had been sucked out of the room. I was just about ready to give Claude a big round of applause for that performance, but then I caught the look on Jaime's face and my smile slowly faded.

An exclamation of *"What the fuck just happened?"* would have been appropriate in the circumstances, but I could see from the set of Jaime's lips and the way that she was making the clocking noise in her mouth the way she always did when she was thinking deeply, that she was way beyond that.

There are four stages of rage and Jaime paid a brief visit to each one in a matter of seconds. The first one was the standard "I'm going to fucking kill you"; the second was a more fitting "I'm going to murder you slowly and painfully"; the third was the macabre "I'm going to dance on your corpse after I've murdered you and eaten your eyeballs,"; and the fourth stage was the nuclear option of "I'm going to murder you so thoroughly there won't be a corpse to dance on." There was a moment as she reached a fifth rarely-seen stage: *"fuck your life"*.

She looked from me to Claude and then back again, then held out her hand.

"You scared two armed thugs into running away with a piece of paper? Let me see the card," Jaime demanded.

"I can't do that Jaime."

"Can't or won't?"

"Won't."

"Fuck you, Claude. *Fuck* you." Jaime wheeled on me. "Tell me something that is not a lie," she demanded.

"I love you," I said after too long a moment.

"And I love you, Bob," Jaime whispered hoarsely, "more than you'll ever know."

"Jaime--" Claude began, and Jaime wheeled on him, directing all of her fury on him.

"You don't get to talk to me Claude! I don't even know who the fuck you are anymore!"

Claude's face went white, and he stepped back, shaken. He had always been able to talk his way out of anything and it shook me to see him speechless in the face of Jaime's wrath.

I stepped forward, imploring, knowing what was coming, knowing it was already done, but I had to try anyway.

"Jaime, don't," I pleaded. "I'm the one who fucked up. Claude wouldn't have to save my ass if I hadn't fucked up this badly. This is all me."

She looked up at me and took a deep breath.

"I know it was," she said, tears in her eyes. "Which is why I have to leave."

Jaime spun and strode toward the door. Claude moved back to give her room to pass, but she didn't even look at him. He glanced at me, pain in his eyes and I nodded slowly, my heart breaking with Jaime's every step.

It was over.

My heart stopped a little when Jaime paused at the broken door.

"Bob?"

"Yes, Jaime?"

"You two deserve each other," she said.

And then Jaime was gone.

There was silence for a long moment, then--

Claude dug into the paper bag, the crackling of the paper loud in the silence. After a moment, he produced two greasy yellow-paper-wrapped sandwiches and threw one to me. I immediately took it and threw it against the wall in a fit of pique.

"How can you eat at a time like this?" I asked as Claude tore into his sandwich, glaring angrily into the distance.

"As bad as things may seem, I've never had a breakfast sandwich let me down," Claude observed.

"It is a tasty sandwich," I agreed. I considered the sandwich on the floor, still mostly in its wrapper. My stomach growled at me, and I swore under my breath, then snatched it up.

If this was a romcom, I would have gotten the girl and the sandwich while making some droll remark about breakfast being the most important meal of the day. We would all laugh and life would be great and nobody would say a word about how Claude was a scary motherfucker who had just defeated two drug dealers with nothing but a business card, because that kind of shit doesn't happen.

But my life wasn't a romcom, and instead, I was reassembling my busted floor-sandwich and wondering how it had all gone wrong. To be honest, if it was a movie, it would be more of a buddy-comedy, maybe with less comedy at the moment.

I really want to say something pithy and snappy here, but I'm just gonna say fuck it.

Roll credits.

Pro Tip for Humans #11:
Tuesdays suck. Don't argue with me here: it's true.

Chapter 3
THIS AIN'T NO CHICK FLICK

Smash cut to me, six months later, standing in an alley outside the open emergency exit door of my workplace, the Porn Emporium—where your kinkiest sex fantasy could become a reality. Here at the Porn Emporium, we carried not only all your questionably-titled big-tittied DVD favourites, we supplied twelve aisles of sex paraphernalia. If we could package it, stick it in a box, and not have to think about what our customers were going to do with it later, then you're goddamn right we sold it.

After spending the last six months trying and failing spectacularly to get Jaime back, this particular morning I was smoking a joint with Sammy, my co-worker/occasional accomplice in getting-up-to-no-good, while I explained my shiny new plan which was absolutely guaranteed-to-work-this-time. It involved Chick Flicks as an educational resource. Lots and lots of Chick Flicks.

Despite the name 'Sammy,' my coworker was one-hundred percent, *not* a dude, and instead one-hundred percent a five-foot-two punk-rock Chinese girl who didn't take shit from anyone, especially me. It was about twenty minutes to six in the morning so it was still darkish outside. Sammy leaned against the wall mostly in shadow, while I stood at the edge of the light from the open door, which framed a perfect rectangle on the ground.

"So, let me get this straight," Sammy mused as she passed the joint to me, the tip still glowing from Sammy's long pull. "Your whole approach to self-improvement is to watch *Ten Things I Hate About You* and *The Wedding Singer* and every other chick flick from the past twenty years?"

I told you I wasn't kidding about the lots and lots of chick flicks.

Sammy managed to say that entire thing while holding the smoke in. I was impressed as I watched her slowly exhale, the smoke whipped away in seconds by the mini wind-tunnel generated by the alley.

"I actually started out optimistic about the whole thing. Figured I could maybe learn something about how chicks think, you know?"

Sammy just gave me the narrowed eyes of doom that said that if she ever got the tiniest amount of authority over me, she wouldn't hesitate to abuse said authority to fire me on the spot. Just because she could.

"Well, first of all, don't fucking call us chicks."

"Duly noted," I agreed as I took a long hit.

Sammy was all punk-rock-goth with artfully torn black fishnet stockings, huge leather boots that gave her an additional two inches of height, a leather mini-shirt, two thick metal-studded leather belts with gigantic buckles and a Misfits t-shirt. All of this under an unbuttoned wool topcoat that clearly wasn't hers, but since it was the closest thing to the door and it was March in Toronto, it was what she was damn well wearing, cuz *you don't fuck with March in Toronto*. If there were any fairy princesses that looked like her, they were ruling their kingdoms from a throne of skulls while Sepultura or Slayer played nonstop.

She technically outranked me since she had worked at the store longer, but we became actual friends once we established the basic rules of working together, which largely involved me *"not fucking up her shit"*, (her words). I worked the graveyard shift, and we had a two-hour window where our schedules crossed in the mornings, so we would usually hang out and shoot the shit. In nicer weather, or on days that looked like the weather wasn't going to completely fuck us up, we usually ended up in the alley, Sammy leaning against the wall while I watched the store through the open door. Somebody had to make sure that nobody was stealing anything, at least not on my shift. Sure it was six in the fucking morning, but the local perverts liked to get their porn early.... or late depending on your perspective.

I continued my point.

"The thing is, the more movies I watched, the more I realized just how fucked up they were. Like every single one. I mean, if you want a blueprint for toxic relationships and unrealistic expectations, well, there it was, all neatly packaged for your easy consumption as a romantic comedy: the quintessential chick-flick."

"Is that the weed talking or are you having a moment?"

I inspected the joint and grinned happily. It *was* pretty good weed.

"Little of both. Rom-coms are fucked up though."

"Rom-coms aren't the same things as chick flicks." Sammy disagreed. "Not even close."

"It is to us guys."

"Philistine."

"Damn skippy," I responded then raised a questioning eyebrow at her. "*You* never took any relationship advice from those movies, right?"

Sammy snatched the joint from me, lips curled in a sour expression of distaste.

"Do I *look* like a fucking frilly pony-riding princess to you?"

I checked her out, just to be sure she wasn't wearing any pink and shook my head because she was clearly looking for a fight.

"Yeah, that was a stupid question," I conceded, "but my point still stands. You just *know* those movies have had some kind of influence over millions of women, and they go into relationships with those expectations. They want the happily-ever-afters, not the happy until whenever the bills are due and one of you can't pay the rent cuz you got laid off."

Sammy gave me a flat look as I passed the joint to her.

"You gonna get all fucking maudlin now and start crying like a little bitch?" she asked.

"Fuck you Sammy. Fuck you in the *ear*." I responded. Something occurred to me. " Who the fuck even uses a word like 'maudlin' anyway?"

"Maybe someone smart like me who knows what the fuck it means?" Sammy sneered. "You *do* know that's not why Jaime walked out on you, right?"

"Yeah, yeah," I grumbled. "I know why she left. Drugs, the threat of being killed, and a whole bunch of etceteras. I'd be a dumbass if I didn't accept my huge fuckup, but it's why she refuses to talk to me at all, that's the part that hurts."

Sammy inhaled deeply on the joint, giving me that probing glare that said she was trying to decide exactly how much of a dumbass I was. I stared back, refusing to break under the pressure of her examination. She suddenly laughed and pointed.

"Ha! I see a tear!" she cackled. "You're totally crying!"

I scowled at her. "You enjoy my pain a little too much; I hope you know that."

"There can never be too much pain," Sammy teased.

"I just want to understand true love. Is that too much to ask."

"Yeah... I don't do true love, or chick flicks, so you're shit outta luck," Sammy mused. "Sorry-not-sorry!"

Sammy turned and walked back into the store, her laughter taunting me. I followed after a moment, pulling the heavy metal door shut behind me. It was getting cold anyway and besides, she was wearing my damn coat.

The Porn Emporium was a decent-sized store with its own parking lot at the side that held a total of six cars. The store also happened to be located in the shadow of the office building where I had worked before being laid off what felt like a lifetime ago.

That alone was an excellent reason for me to work graveyard, since I wouldn't have to accidentally run into any old coworkers who had survived the purge. My regulars tended to be late-night partiers looking to spice up the night, or the occasional porn-enthusiast who just couldn't wait. We didn't do online orders, which meant dealing with customers face-to-face.

Sammy's laughter died down, and now she coughed loudly and obviously, trying to get my attention. I turned to look, and the question on my lips died instantly.

The Boss stood in the middle of the store at the intersection of butt-plugs, dildos and more. There was an awkward-looking white dude with him. If my life had been the movie that I was thoroughly convinced it was, the Boss would be played by Danny DeVito. He was a short, wide, troll of a man, the shiny dome of his bald head poking out of a fringe of hair. Sammy had once said that from the back, his head reminded her of a micro-penis. Since then, I had been unable to get that image out of my head. The Boss was mean-spirited and cheap as hell, but as a boss, he generally didn't give a shit what we did as long as it didn't fuck with his profits.

The Boss's policy on drugs? Don't do them in the store; that's what the alley is for.

"What the fuck are you still doing here, Bobby?" he said, instantly targeting me as he glanced at the gold Rolex on his wrist. "I don't pay overtime, so no tricks from you."

"I was just on my way home--" I protested, heading for my packed knapsack on the counter next to the themed obvious knockoff Lisney Prince condom display from India.

"Since you're here, you might as well meet the new guy," the Boss hooked his thumb over his shoulder at the awkward looking kid standing behind him.

The Boss smirked at Sammy. "Got some new blood for you to train Sammy." He turned to the kid. "New guy, introduce yourself."

The kid stepped forward to meet us, grin on his face, hand outstretched. I glanced at Sammy, who was already making her way out from behind the counter to give him an official welcome.

"I'm Benjamin," he said helpfully and a little too eagerly. I wondered if he had ever seen porn before. The poor guy looked like a Bible class refugee.

I wheeled over the nearby mop-bucket and slapped the handle of the mop into Benjamin's outstretched hand.

"I'm Bob, that's Sammy, and this is the bucket. You and it are going to be the best of friends."

Benjamin blinked rapidly in confusion, the smile on his face fading. Sammy had pulled the same thing on me on my first day of work, and I recognized the look on poor Benjamin's face. He glanced back at the Boss for help, but the Boss was already making his way out of the store, clearly not giving a single flying fuck.

"Booths one and three need a little bit of love," Sammy drawled. "You're going to need gloves."

When I had first seen the booths, my initial thought was, why is everything covered in plastic? I would later find out that one of the downsides of working in a porn shop is the sheer number of bonafide creeps who are paying customers. Some of them like to make creative use of our viewing booths, which are little closed-off closets in the back of the store with some seriously high-quality headphones attached. The Boss was a cheapass, but apparently, he was also an audiophile.

As much fun as it was going to be to watch Benjamin realize what actually happened in the so-called viewing booths in the back of the store, I had a bus to catch.

"Sorry buddy: new guy always gets cleanup," I said with as much compassion as I could dredge up. "Just be glad you're not starting on a Tuesday."

"He's right," Sammy agreed with an evil grin. "You're gonna love Tuesdays."

I made my way to the exit, not even looking back to see the many ways Benjamin was reconsidering his life choices.

"But, it is Tuesday!" Benjamin implored to my departing back.

"Sucks to be you!" I called back cheerfully.

"Hey, Bob!" Sammy called after me, and I paused to look back at her.

"I gotta catch my bus!"

Sammy held up a DVD copy of Sloppy Seconds for Seniors in 3D from the shelf in front of her. Benjamin had gone red in the face, thoroughly scandalized.

"I found some true love for you over in aisle three!"

I shot Sammy the one-fingered salute and turned to leave but was stopped in my tracks. A tall blonde woman with huge black sunglasses on her face had just entered. She took off the sunglasses to reveal a pair of the most stunning blue eyes I had ever seen, and then bit suggestively on one of the arms of the sunglasses. Blondie winked mischievously, giving me a sultry and knowing smile.

The thought that this gorgeous woman in the long fur coat and too short mini-skirt with those fuck-me boots had just witnessed that display would have ordinarily put me off my stride, but not this morning. This morning I had a bus to catch.

"So sorry, " I mumbled and exited the store at a run, determined to catch my bus.

I glanced toward the sky where the sun was trying to decide whether to make an appearance. Tuesday or not, it looked like it was going to be a damn good day, I mean, at least it wasn't me holding the goddamn mop.

Tips for Humans #373:
Don't be the crazy one.

Chapter 4
JAIME'S INFINITE PLAYLIST

Iwaited until I was on the bus before I put in my headphones
and opened iTunes, telling myself that *this morning
would be different goddamit; this morning I would be
not a borderline stalker, and maybe the one thing I was
looking forward to and dreading at the same time, wasn't
even there anyway,* but like all of the other times over the past
four weeks, I was wrong.

Of course, it was there on the screen, the title saying everything
that it needed to get my complete interest. Taunting me.

Jaime's Infinite Playlist.

My hands shook from the rush of adrenaline as I greedily
scrolled through the list of songs that my ex-girlfriend had
recently listened to on her own phone. By some fluke of
technology, it showed up on my iTunes. It was just like an addict
getting his fix, now that I think of it. I paused, savouring the
moment, that heady rush of anticipation ready to rush over me
and fill me with unimaginable bliss. I would have drunk from
that anticipation if I could, taken it and injected it into my veins
and let myself drown any guilt that might have wanted to come
out and play.

I knew it was bad, but goddamn it was so, so *good.*

I hit PLAY.

Seriously, what did you expect from the guy who snorts heroin? Some kind of restraint?

Radiohead filled my ears, assuring me that *everything was in its right place, right place,* and I leaned my head against the glass, trying to lose myself for a while. For a moment it became the soundtrack for my life, perfectly in time with the hypnotic rock and sway of the bus as it carried us denizens of the graveyard shift into the waiting dawn. The lumbering vehicle rumbled smoothly from stop to start, the thrum of the engine vibrating through my entire being. My body moved in time with the sway as the bus navigated the bumps and potholes and demonstrated how few fucks it gave, because it was the goddamn morning bus and nothing got in its way.

I usually traveled in silent solidarity with the few passengers, enjoying one of the side-benefits of working the graveyard shift: watching the city awaken. All along the route, lights were switched on, others switched off as people left their houses. There was a general sense of the city itself stretching and yawning, preparing for the business of the day. It was strangely comforting knowing that my day had ended and now it was someone else's turn. Most mornings I would lean my head against the window, music in my ears, witness to the secret life of a city half-awake.

The unseasoned passenger would have been lulled into sleep, the kind of sleep that had made lesser men miss their stops on countless occasions, but I was the mutha-fuckin' master of the graveyard shift, and besides, I had Jaime on my mind.

Like any reasonable person, you're probably looking at me in absolute horror and a mixture of disgust usually reserved for politicians and pineapple on pizza, but in my defence, *you would have done it too*, and pineapple is awesome on pizza, *so bring it!*

"What's on the playlist this morning?" a woman's voice pierced through my chill vibe, right in my ear.

I'll be honest: I almost jumped out of my skin. I was yanked out of the semi-hypnotic state I had fallen into, slight panic and guilt flooding me as I turned from staring out the window to find the face of Crazy Mary inches from my own.

"Hello, Crazy Mary," I said, pulling out one earbud as I shifted in my seat. I tried to appear as nonplussed as possible. She had scared the shit out of me, but I was still enjoying a mellow high from the weed I had smoked earlier with Sammy, so 'nonplussed' was pretty easy for me to pull off.

After a year of riding on the 6:15 AM #2 bus I recognized a lot of the recurring characters in this strange movie that my life had become. It didn't matter the time of year, they always boarded the bus at their same stops along the Bloor line. I didn't know their names of course, so I just made up names for everybody. The group of Filipino maids that boarded at Yonge and Bloor were the Four Sandras; the tall skinny Kenyan guy in the blue overalls I referred to as Ken; the short blonde girl who had an amazing smile and was always deep in her law journals was Reese; and the older black lady in her sixties who always wore what seemed to be about 80% of her wardrobe on her body, whose face, currently three inches from my own, was Crazy Mary, but in my defence, in her case she told me that was her name.

Crazy Mary's halitosis was particularly vile this morning, and I almost gagged on the cloud of garlic that threatened to overtake my senses and melt my brain to a puddle of garlic overload.

"Holy shit, what have you been *eating*?" I managed to gasp, one finger pressed against the front of my nostrils.

"It's garlic! Gotta keep them vampires at bay!" Crazy Mary noticed my reaction and glared at me, squinting suspiciously. "You ain't one of them are you? You ain't got the eyes but still..."

"Not even close, but if I was, your breath would be the perfect weapon."

"Ain't no vampire bit me yet, so it's working," Crazy Mary said happily.

"Oh, it's definitely working," I gagged. "A little too well."

Garlic breath pummelled my senses as Crazy Mary huffed in

my direction. "You'd tell me if you was a vampire, wouldn't you Bobby?" she asked intently.

"I swear if I ever turn into a vampire that I'll be sure and mention it," I managed. "Can you stop breathing on me now? Please?"

Crazy Mary relented and pulled back, head bopping to her own internal music. She gave me a knowing smile and tilted her head to my headphones.

"So what's the girlfriend listening to this morning?"

"She seems to be into Radiohead these days," I replied. I had told Crazy Mary about the playlist one morning. "She's out of her Blue October phase, so she might be mellowing a little." Blue October had been seriously angry and intense, even for me.

"What you getting outta it anyway? Ain't like you're going to suddenly know what makes her tick from her music," Crazy Mary said smugly. "Might as well figure out how women think first."

I looked at Crazy Mary expectantly, waiting for her to finish the thought.

"And exactly how do I do *that?*" I prompted.

"Ain't nobody knows," she grinned. "That's crazy talk. Like you and that dang playlist."

"It's just a playlist," I insisted. "It's nothing. Just a way for me to feel closer to her, you know?"

Crazy Mary rolled her eyes, not buying what I was selling. Typical. If it had been Claude he would have totally understood what I was saying, not just because he was a dude, but because he was my bro, mi amigo, totally on the same wavelength and he always had my back.

"You know it's wrong no matter how much you want to pretty it up," she said, leaning away from me as if I was the crazy person.

I sighed, hating that Crazy Mary was right. But I knew what I was doing, and if there was anything I had learned from watching six-months' worth of chick-flicks, it was that Lloyd Dobler grand gestures only worked in the movies. Listening to

Jaime's playlist might have made me *feel* closer to Jaime, but it was a one-sided closeness. She wasn't listening to music to send some message out to the universe, it was just her way of coping, and there I was, eavesdropping like an asshole.

I looked out the window, realizing where we were and it was like time slowed to a crawl.

The problem with my route home was that it passed by the one place on earth that filled me with equal amounts of excitement and dread without the benefit of being a shitty theme park or shoddily constructed horror house. It was the place that made my heart want to thump its way out of my chest and the butterflies burst from my gut in a carnivorous rage. It was the place that made me want to take a bus forty minutes out of my way to avoid.

It was Jaime's apartment.

The location of Jaime's apartment had been one of the coincidental perks when we had been dating, almost as if we were neighbours, apart by barely a half-kilometre, but that proximity had come back to bite me in the ass really fucking hard. Every morning as the bus approached her stop, I tried to close my eyes and think about something else until we passed a safe distance away.

Some mornings I peeked, even though it was too early for Jaime to be up, but I peeked anyway, hoping to somehow catch a glimpse of her. Hope is made for fools after all. Most times, I made it through without ugly crying. *Most* times.

I stared at the nearby door, fighting the urge to stand up and push the red stop button on the pole ahead of me. I curled my hand into a fist, willing myself to stay seated, telling myself that it wasn't worth the trouble it would bring. It was a familiar battle especially when I was at my lowest and all I had to do was make it through the intersection. If the bus stopped on the corner, the urge would be too much to fight--

The bus sailed past the stop and through the intersection, heading steadily on its Eastbound route.

I let out a sigh of relief and sank back into my seat, celebrating my small victory.

I hadn't gotten off.

This is a big fucking deal, so let me just say it again in case you didn't get it the first time: *I didn't get off*. Instead, I smiled tightly, feeling the sting of tears behind my eyes, and dug into my coat pocket.

"I got something for you," I said and Crazy Mary's eyes lit up like it was Christmas, and it was her turn to French-kiss Old Saint Nick. I dug into my coat pocket, fingers navigating past a bundle of receipts and into the hole at the bottom that had defied my rudimentary sewing skills. Anything heavy automatically dropped through that hole and into the lining of the coat, so I usually avoided that pocket. I found what I was looking for and held up the two Snickers bars between us. Crazy Mary grinned wildly and plucked one of them out of my hand. She gleefully unwrapped the candy bar and shoved it into her mouth as if she hadn't eaten in days. She stopped chewing and looked at me with concern.

"You ain't gonna eat with me?" she said through an open mouthful of missing teeth, peanuts, and sticky nougat that I wished I hadn't seen.

"Yeah, sure," I agreed and unwrapped my candy. I made sure to always pick up two Snickers ever since my first encounter with Mary, when she'd asked to share mine. It turns out that she didn't like to eat alone as much as I didn't like not having a Snickers to eat.

Crazy Mary cackled. "Still sure you ain't no vampire?"

"One hundred percent," I said and bit into my Snickers.

Crazy Mary resumed devouring her treat. I had tried giving her a Mars bar once, and she had accepted it, but definitely not as eagerly as the Snickers.

She was the one variable that made taking the bus home an adventure, since I could never predict when she would show up, and then when she did, I never saw her coming. It was like she had ninja powers that she saved just for sneaking up on me.

The familiar strum of guitars filled my left ear as the *Foo Fighters* prepared to tell me hello and about how they had waited for me, *Everlong.*

Jaime had our *song on her playlist..*

It was as if a sharp, white-hot bolt of lightning had struck through my earbud and right into my goddamn heart.

"Holy fucknuts!"

My heart thumping harder than I had felt in a long time. Without a thought, I jumped up and rang the bell. Crazy Mary reflexively scooted over to the empty seat across the aisle, but she was clearly not happy about it. Her head whipped back and forth as she desperately searched for an obvious solution to what was bugging me, her frown more severe as she couldn't find one.

"Hey, where you going? This ain't your stop Bobby!"

"I gotta run an errand," I lied as I staggered toward the door. "See you later!"

"You're a shit liar!"

"I know!" I shrugged. The bus coasted to a stop, and the back doors opened, allowing me to avoid Crazy Mary's judgmental stare. Like a crazy old lady with missing teeth and garlic-breath had any right to criticize. I watched the bus drive away into the early morning traffic and plugged in my other earbud. *The Foo Fighters* filled my world, and I might have sung along to the chorus as I turned and shambled back down the street. The sun was already spreading its warm light across the tops of a few of the taller buildings as my feet fell into rhythm with the steady thump-thump-thump of my wildly beating heart.

I was heading toward Jaime, going to answer the call she had so obviously put out to the universe.

It was *our* song.

Pro-Tip for Humans #34:
True friends are the ones digging you out of that crater you just dug for yourself.

Chapter 5
SIC TRANSIT GLORIA

Just so you know, I kinda-sorta chickened out on the whole damn thing. Like *big* time.

I was doing this weird half-walk that was more like a hesitant run, each step in time with the Foo Fighters blasting in my ears, taking me back down the block, closer to Jaime. The thing that I hadn't considered was that these were three very long blocks, and by the time I reached the end of the first block, the music had already changed. It was the music change that did it for me, going from the hopeful and triumphant sounds of *Everlong*, and moving to the mocking and sarcastic lyrics of *My Own Worst Enemy*. My steps became less sure, doubt raising its ugly head and punching me squarely in the nuts as *I asked myself what the fuck was I actually doing?* All of the bravado I had previously possessed spontaneously said *"fuck it"* and stumbled away to get drunk with my pride.

By the time I reached the end of the block and taken refuge from the sudden wind that the universe had whipped up just to fuck with me, I had fumbled my phone out and called the one person who could tell me how much of an idiot I was being and save me from myself..

"That's a bit dramatic even for you, don't you think?" Louise said.

"Well, of *course,* it's dramatic," I muttered, eyeing the clutch of commuters neatly queued at the bus stop. "I'm in crisis here, Louise. That's why I called you."

Louise was my female best friend. Yes, Claude was my main best friend, but while he and I could talk about the fine details and philosophy of Olympic Curling, even if we had no interest in it, and we could even pick up in the middle of conversations after going months without seeing each other, we never actually talked about *anything of substance.* He knew how to be there for me when there was a problem, but we never discussed the actual problem. That was where Louise came in. Claude could tell me I was a dumbass, Louise was the one who listened to me whine and told me *why* I was a dumbass. And she did it with a British accent, which made my dumbassery so much more obvious.

Louise was also the one who had introduced me to Jaime. She hadn't meant to, but it was just one of those things that happened. Kinda like how true love can never be denied or something like that. Like fate or whatever.

"Go home, Bob," Louise sighed, in that very British way she had. Even her sigh had an accent.

Jaime chose that moment to walk around the corner, her familiar mop of curls bouncing as she made her way to the bakery, and my heart stopped, an idiot smile spreading across my face as I drank in the euphoria that always came from seeing her.

The telltale white cord leading to her ears indicated that she was listening to her music, maybe even the same song I was listening to. All of my worries seemed to fade as I looked at her, admiring her effortless grace. Watching from a distance, I could properly appreciate how goddamn perfect my ex-girlfriend was.

I never properly described Jaime before, so here goes: she was about five-foot-six with the kind of lean muscle lots of girls only wished for and that she made a point of going to the gym regularly to attain. Remember that whole army stint that I mentioned earlier? She had kept up her workout and training routine in the four years since she had left the army, so it was that kind of muscle. She was half-white, half-black, with the kind of indefinable beauty that a lot of people just ended up labelling as exotic, mostly because of the impossibly thick lustrous curls that framed her face. She was dressed in a cautious combination of jeans and wool-coat that probably hid a sweater underneath because like most Torontonians, she knew how to dress in layers, never trusting the weather not to completely fuck her over.

"I just want her to *talk* to me. Even a hello would be nice. We were together for a year, and now it feels like it meant *nothing* to her... like *I* meant nothing to her, you know?"

"Please allow me to counter your eloquent argument with two facts. A. you're whinging. B. the restraining order," Louise insisted passionately since Brits don't actually yell. "She will have you arrested!"

I looked away from Louise in indignation as Jaime entered the Bakery and Coffee Shop.

"I'm not whinging," I whined.

"Definitely sounds like whinging to me," Louise quipped. "You have been watching Rom-Coms again, haven't you?"

"If I lied and said no, would you believe me?"

"I'm putting this conversation out of its misery Bob. Tell me you're going home."

"Could you at least talk to her about me? She still listens to you."

"Let me think about it."

"Great—"

"I thought about it, and the answer is no."

"'Hello, customer service?'" I feigned a call. "'This friend is defective, and I'd like to return her.'"

"You know you love me. Now go home, Bob. *Click!*'"

I glared at the phone and then sighed deeply, realizing how right she was.

"Bye, Louise," I mumbled.

I glanced around at the queue of people, and then leaned against the glass wall of the bus shelter. I occasionally glanced across the street at the Bakery and Coffee Shop, waiting for Jaime to make a reappearance with her coffee and bagel.

Bzzt! A text message alert popped up on my phone.

Claude: *Hey, dude, you wanna grab some breakfast?*

I shrugged and considered, then typed my response.

Me: *Sure? I'm on the bus now. Just passing Islington.*

Someone stepped in front of me, blocking my view. I looked up, preparing some choice words of a what-the-fuck nature, but I froze when I saw who was deliberately blocking me.

"Isn't Islington two blocks that way?" Claude asked, pointing in the wrong direction. "I might have to run to catch up with your bus, but I think I can handle it."

"Fuck," I swore again for emphasis.

Look, I'm going to save some time here, okay? You should always assume that Claude is dressed in a suit of some kind, mostly without a tie. Think of what you expect a movie star to look like on the cover of GQ magazine, and that's Claude. The topcoat he wore had a very expensive-looking weave that made my wallet hide in embarrassment. Dressed like that, he should have looked completely out of place in this neighbourhood, but as always, he managed to pull it off. He looked utterly at home, no matter where he was.

Claude had a disposable cup of steaming coffee in his hand, the logo of the Bakery and Coffee Shop proudly proclaiming where he had made his purchase.

"Louise totally called you, didn't she?" I asked in disbelief. "*How the hell did you even get here so fast?*"

"Funny story: I missed you at the store, so I was trying to catch up with your bus," Claude said casually as if I wasn't wearing my guilt all over my face. "You'll never guess who I saw jump out of that bus and make his way back to his ex-girlfriend's corner. I'll give you two guesses," Claude said. He paused to sip his coffee and peered at me over the lid. "Hint: rhymes with Bob, looks like you."

The bus chose that moment to arrive, and I stepped out of line to let the real commuters stream past, some of them shooting narrowed eyes of irritation at me.

"I could say something totally cliche like 'this isn't what it looks like' if it makes you feel better?" I suggested.

"Go for it."

"This isn't what it looks like?" I ventured.

"Well that's a relief," Claude said. "For a second there, I thought you were stalking your ex-girlfriend."

"Keep your voice down!" I hissed, but a couple of the **commuters** had heard him and now glared at both of us. "Besides, it's not *really* stalking." I clasped my hands together and tried to look as saintly as possible. "I'm just making sure she's *okay*."

"Seriously, dude?"

"Well she's been listening to this really sad playlist--" I stopped and swallowed my words, realizing what I had just admitted to when Claude immediately looked at my phone. "Shit."

Claude sighed deeply and held out his hand.

"Give it. Now."

I reflexively pulled my phone away, caressing it to my chest.

"Dude," Claude said warningly.

"Dude yourself!" I replied. "You're going to log me out, and I don't think I can handle that right now."

Claude nodded in understanding and shrugged. "Just gimme the phone, Bob," he said softly.

"I thought you were on my side!" I protested.

"I *am* on your side!" Claude hissed. "That's why I'm here trying to stop you from doing something stupid!" He paused. "Again!"

The bus trundled away into the slow-moving traffic, leaving us alone in the glass enclosure. We wouldn't be alone for long; more commuters were already on their way to the bus stop. Claude and I both glanced across the street at the Eastbound bus stop, but Jaime wasn't there yet.

"I'm your *friend,* Bob, I can't just sit around and watch you shoot yourself in the face. Somebody's gotta save you from yourself."

I thought about it and slumped in defeat.

"You're right, dude," I finally muttered. "It *is* a little creepy."

"I would have said *'a lot'* creepy, but that works too."

"In my defence, I didn't go looking for it. I logged in one day, and there it was: 'Jaime's Mega-Sad Playlist.' It was like fate. How could I not listen to it?"

"Yeah ... I'm just gonna upgrade you to 'Definitely Creepy,' totally free of charge since we're such old friends," Claude said. There was that damned hand again. "Now!"

"I'll do it myself," I muttered in protest and defeat as I held up the phone and tapped my way to Settings.

Movement from across the street caught my eye. Jaime had exited the Bakery and Coffee Shop, coffee and bagel in hand, but she wasn't alone. A tall, strikingly-handsome guy with a man-purse slung over his shoulder, followed closely, big cheesy grin on his stupidly handsome face. He had hair that could only be described as "lustrous." I hated that motherfucker on sight, especially when Jaime looked back and smiled up at him in the same way she had always looked at me, her big brown eyes drinking in all of him—

I turned away, heart dully pounding in my ears, not wanting to see.

Claude looked from me to Jaime and then back to me again.

"They're kissing, aren't they?" I asked.

Claude's face twisted as he considered lying. "No... not really... okay, yeah, they're kissing, but maybe they're just really, really good friends?"

I slapped the phone into Claude's outstretched hand and took off, determined not to look back, blinking back the hot sting of tears.

"We should go now," I said over my shoulder to Claude, and somehow I managed not to choke on the words as I stumbled away.

"Good idea," Claude said. "Except the car is this way."

I don't even remember how we got back to the car. All I could see playing over and over in my head was Jaime looking up at that douchebag and pulling close to kiss him.

I am proud to say I didn't look back. I didn't do something stupid like try to pick a fight with the dude kissing Jaime and try to rearrange his face with my fist so he couldn't go around kissing people's ex-girlfriends like that. I didn't do anything like that at all. This story would have a completely different ending if I had done that.

Pro-Tip for Humans #86:
Bartenders are not your fucking therapists.

Chapter 6
CONFESSIONS, BARS, AND OTHER LIES

The Rock Bottom bar was the shitty hole-in-the-wall bar around the corner from my apartment, the diviest of dives and the perfect place to drown your sorrows and/or a broken heart at nine in the morning, mostly due to the fact that it was close by and that it was open.

If you're one of those people who thinks that day-drinking at 9 AM is way too early, please feel free to fuck off, or go and get your heart ripped out, stomped on, shredded, and fed to you, and *then* we can talk. Once you've done that, I may even pour you some of what I'm having and we can drink together and you can listen to how Jaime had—

"— Stuck her *fucking tongue down that guy's throat* and practically fucked him in public like that!" I complained.

The bartender stopped pouring the whiskey into my glass and shrugged. "Bitches, right?"

Claude was already shaking his head in disagreement. "Nope! Did not happen that way. He's exaggerating. Bob, tell him you're exaggerating."

"She's *not* a bitch," I protested. "She's the love of my life. But! She might as well have been fucking that guy in public," I protested. "It *feels* like that's what she was doing."

Randy was what the bartender called himself, but I kinda got the idea that it wasn't his actual name. He was a big white guy, scruffy beard, lots of tattoos and had a scar about six-inches long on the right side of his face from his hairline to right beneath his earlobe. Looking at him, you got the idea that he was not to be fucked with, but he was a bit of a softie if he decided he liked you.

"You shoulda fucked that guy up," Randy said matter-of-factly and then poured me an extra finger of whiskey.

"I think that goes against every rom-com rule in existence," Claude said unconvincingly while I took the glass and drank before Randy could change his mind about pouring me a little extra.

"I don't think we're watching the same movie then," Randy smirked at Claude. "Damn girl broke his heart man. Somebody's gotta pay."

I slammed the glass on the bar. "Fuck yeah!"

Randy helpfully poured a refill and then tipped the bottle in Claude's direction. I was on my fourth glass, and Claude was still on his first.

"And that right there is exactly why you don't ask your bartender for advice on your love life," Claude pointed out.

"I'm just here to pour the drinks and take your money," Randy smirked. "The bad advice is on the house."

The alcohol was having the desired effect, and I was no longer feeling as fucked-up about Jaime as I had been, but that was only because I wasn't actually thinking about her non-stop. In fact, there were entire minutes that I didn't even think of her and her perfect lips. There was still a stab of pain and that queasiness in my gut every time I pictured Jaime kissing Fuck-face-with-the-perfect-hair, but at least my hands had stopped balling into painful fists in search of somebody to punch.

"Why doesn't she love me?" I implored Claude.

"Oh, she loves you, but she's just not *in* love with you anymore."

"You really aren't helping."

"I'm buying the drinks," Claude pointed out.

"I stand corrected!" I slammed my glass down for a refill, which Randy happily poured. "You help in the most helpful way!"

"Damn skippy," Claude said, draining his whiskey with a grimace.

"So…" I said as casually as possible, and judging from Claude's suspicious look, it wasn't casual in the slightest, "can we stop at my place?"

"No drugs!"

"But—"

"Whatever you're about to say is a lie."

"Nonono, wait… maybe… okay: definitely yes.'

Claude stood, located the bathroom at the end of the bar and pointed to it. "We're going to get some food into you, but first I'm going to hit the head."

I opened my mouth to warn him about the bathroom but then the petty side of me decided that the man stopping me from getting my drugs didn't deserve the heads up. I held my tongue and tried to drown it in booze instead.

Claude turned to the bartender. "Please don't sell him any drugs. I'm not paying for them."

Pettiness validated.

I waited for Claude to walk away before I shot a sly look at Randy. "So about those drugs?"

Randy shook his head. "Cash only. Especially from you."

"So that's a no?"

"This one's on the house," Randy said as he poured.

"Well, at least it's *one* way to get fucked up." I took the glass and drank quickly, turning on the wobbly stool to observe Claude's return from the bathroom.

"Why didn't you give me the heads-up about the bathroom?"

Randy chortled like a 90's teenager in an AC/DC t-shirt. "He said 'head.'"

"Some things have to be experienced first hand," I quipped and got to my feet, swaying a tiny bit. "My turn." I solemnly saluted Claude and Randy. "I may be a while."

I made my way into the darkened depths of the bar, footsteps creaking hollowly on the old wood floors. There was a tall man in the very back of the bar and it was as if the shadows wrapped themselves around him, but I glanced away before I became too curious. I had a plan and didn't need any distractions. My heart beat dully with each step as an escape plan formulated itself in my drunken mind, and *yes, it was a good plan, why wouldn't it be?* Just sneak out the back and then down the block to my apartment before Claude was any the wiser. I'd be high as a kite before he realized I was gone.

I almost looked back when I reached the stairs, but didn't want to look too guilty. Like most bar and restaurant bathrooms in Toronto, this bathroom lived in the basement, so I had to navigate the too-narrow staircase that could only fit one person at a time and was hell to manage on a busy night. There was a single light at the bottom of the stairs and *of course* it flickered badly as if threatening darkness at any moment, just you wait and see.

The sign clearly said MEN'S and and helpfully pointed to the left away from the door that was marked WOMEN'S, but I already knew exactly where to go. The urge to urinate had come on pretty strong, and I was practically doing the pee dance by the time I hit the landing. I rushed through the door at the end, unzipping as I walked since there was nobody around, and shouldering open the door, rushed to the urinal at the back, ready to release a stream of pee with the force of a firehose. Relief flooded through me, and I relaxed enough to realize that there was somebody else inside the grimy bathroom with me.

An impossibly huge gorilla of a man glared at me from over at the sink, his eyes an intense light blue that seemed to burn in his sockets. I had time to wonder what it was that I had done to piss me off, but then I saw he was holding another man against the wall by the neck, but that was not the worst of it. The gorilla was in the process of ripping the incisors out of the other man's head with a pair of rusty old pliers, and there was blood everywhere.

"You got a problem?" the gorilla snarled, and I noticed how impossibly long his incisors were. They looked more like fangs than anything else.

I looked away in a hurry, suddenly terrified, heart pounding, convinced that I was about to be murdered while urinating, and that was going to be embarrassing. I managed to force myself to stop peeing, zipped up in a hurry and got the fuck out of there, deliberately not looking at the two men.

The screams started as soon as the door closed behind me. I hesitated, asking myself if I really wanted to get involved, then decided that I should let Randy know what was going on. The lights chose that moment to flicker out, and I was left in darkness, the only light coming from the crack around the bathroom door and from down the stairwell.

That's when I became convinced that there was someone in the dark with me. The hairs on my arms rose in response and a cold terror coiled in my gut--

A shadow fell across the stairwell as someone made their way down the stairs, thud... thud... thud... and all at once I *knew* it wasn't Randy or Claude coming to see what was taking so long. It was someone terrible, something bad—

I ran as if my life depended on it, rushing through the darkness toward the back of the bar to the stairs that I knew were there. All I had to do was to get to the stairs and get the fuck out into the sunlight and I would be safe. I knew this, felt it deep in my gut.

I pushed through the doors, seeing the waiting sunlight, convinced that I was not going to make it, that some clawed hand would reach out and snag me back into the dark, but nothing of the sort happened. The doors opened, and I stumbled out, falling onto the ground, and only then did I turn. The stairwell was empty.

Claude leaned arrogantly against the alley wall. He didn't even have the courtesy to be out of breath.

"Did you fucking teleport or something?" I gaped at him in

utter amazement.

"What the fuck just happened? Is someone after you?"

I glanced at the empty stairwell and remembered the look on the big gorilla's face. That was a man you did not fuck with. I had seen all kinds of rough types in the Rock Bottom, but this was the first time I had ever been terrified of actually being murdered where I stood. It was like the boogey man had shown up. And what the fuck was the deal with the pliers anyway? *Was he pulling that man's teeth out?* I shook my head, trying to clear the memories, for some reason scared to tell Claude about what I had seen.

"It's nothing, really," I lied. "Weird dude jacking off in the restroom."

"Did you get lost trying to ditch me?"

I shrugged trying to regain my composure. "Can you blame me?"

Claude rolled his eyes.

"Let's get outta here," I said, with a glance toward the stairs. "You mentioned buying me food, so let's do that." I walked toward the mouth of the alley, a perplexed Claude falling into step with me.

"So we're going to just ignore the fact that you were trying to ditch me to go get drugs?" Claude asked.

I was just glad that we were getting as far from the bar as possible, but didn't want to show Claude how freaked out I was. I glanced at him in irritation. "Well, you were willing to buy me enough drinks to black out an elephant, but you won't let me get my *drugs*. You *do* realize that either way, I'd still be getting fucked up, right?"

"Look, dude, you feel like shit, and I get that you want to indulge in a little bit of self-destruction. I get it," Claude said. "Completely. So I'm letting you be an idiot for a while, just not an idiot with a future at the morgue."

"Thanks?"

"But the problem with self-destruction is that sometimes you don't know when to stop. And Bob, *you never know when to stop,* and that scares the shit out of me, man."

I wanted to say something comforting, but my mind kept going back to the men in the bathroom and I shuddered. Claude seemed to think that was in response to his words. He reached out to grab my shoulder.

"You're my best friend, Bob. I'm not going to let you kill yourself." Claude said. "I'm not going to be the one to have to call your mom and tell her you died of an overdose. Don't do that to me, man. I'm not strong enough to handle that."

I looked at Claude for a long moment and then said, "What would you say if I told you that there was a dude pulling out another dude's teeth with a fricking pliers in the bathroom?"

Claude raised an eyebrow, quickly assessing if I was joking and when he realized that I wasn't, he took my arm and quickly led me away from the alley. "We're going to get the hell out of here before he comes looking for you, and then you're not going to come back to this bar, like ever again."

"But the cheap drinks--"

"Do you want to end up in a bathroom with that same dude pulling your teeth out?"

"I'm never coming back to this bar!" I vowed.

"Glad we can agree on something."

As we drove away from the Rock Bottom, I got a glimpse of the exit doors in the alley where a large figure in black exited very deliberately and seemed to *look right at me.* It was just for a moment, and then we were out of sight of each other, but from the way the hair stood up on my arm again, I got a sense that I had dodged a very large bullet.

And maybe a pair of pliers.

Pro-Tip for Humans #44:
Your friends have their own secret lives.

Chapter 7
THE TALENTED MR. SMITH

We made our way to the Thompson Diner, located on the southern side of Bathurst, tucked inside the downstairs corner of the Thompson Hotel. It had a so-called "all-American" aesthetic as if designed by a slightly drunk Canadian who had never actually stepped foot inside a real diner and had only seen them in movies or on tv. The diner was the perfect place to get stinking drunk *and* well-fed. The bartender poured heavy, and the helpings had been American-sized from the beginning.

The Thompson housed some of the Hollywood elite who came into town for the Toronto International Film Festival, so the designer had gone all out in case any of the movie stars wanted to grab a little breakfast or hang out for a while. As a result, there was a 60's vibe to the decor, all polished aluminum and plush leather seats in the enormous American-sized booths. It was a pity that those movie stars tended to avoid the diner itself unless they were massively drunk in the middle of the night and wanted a huge stack of thick Thompson Diner (™) Waffles with that special Canadian Maple Syrup. The better to soak up the booze you see.

It was busy with at least ten people waiting when we arrived, but Claude and I were immediately shown to a booth as if we were some kind of VIPs. The benefit of hanging with Claude is that he never had to wait in lines. There were lots of men in light-coloured suits seated with moderately-attractive women in moderately-attractive business attire. I had no doubt when they left they would all be wearing some version of the wool topcoats that made this time of year in the city look like a scene from the Matrix.

The tinny strains of *Sic Transit Gloria* floated from the speakers, the lyrics barely audible over the hum and clatter of early-morning diners. I knew the song well enough to bob my head in time, but didn't know the words well enough to do more than mumble.

"I used to love this song," I murmured and turned back to Claude.

"But then Jaime ruined it for you?" Claude finished my sentence.

I glared at him, all of the drama draining out of my revelation. "... but then Jaime ruined it for me."

Claude grinned at the waiting waiter, a slim nerdy-looking guy with a name tag that declared *Hi! My Name is JIMMY*.

"Hi, 'My Name is Jimmy!' He's going to have the Big Breakfast Special, extra side of bacon, a glass of Jack with no ice ... and a side of ennui."

"I was hoping for a side of True Love," I muttered.

"Sorry, sir," Jimmy stuttered, "we're fresh out of True Love." He paused and blushed. "Sorry about that."

"Bring the whiskey first, and keep 'em coming," I instructed. Jimmy shuffled away and I directed my attention to Claude. "You *are* drinking with me, right?"

"*You* can get as fucked up as you want," Claude said wryly, "but somebody's got to drive."

"Oh, come on! That's what Uber is for."

"You do realize it's only ten-thirty in the morning, right?"

"For someone in your profession, you don't party as much as I hoped you would." I stage-whispered to him and grinned sloppily. Yes, I was still drunk and really looking forward to the next drink, so I was exaggerating my movements, and even though I knew I was doing it, I couldn't seem to stop myself. It was *that* kind of a buzz.

Claude piled the little packets of jam on top of each other, making a pyramid. It was just one of the things he did, making those perfect little pyramids, that I would inevitably knock over just because I could.

"Guys in my profession get arrested and go to jail a lot," Claude said as he started a second row of jam bricks. "Some of them even get killed, and it's because they get sloppy. Wanna know how they get sloppy?"

"They party a lot and get fucked up?" I ventured a drunken guess.

"Have I told you this story before? Doesn't matter, cuz you're right. They party a lot and get fucked up." Claude finished his construction and looked at me with a wry smile. "You want to know what the cops call me?"

"I'm going to go with 'John Smith,'" I said cockily.

Claude shook his head. I interrupted before he could speak, enjoying the game I called *"Annoy the Shit out of Claude."*

"'Hey you, stop?'"

Nope.

"'Also Known As?'"

Nope.

"'Didja see—"

Claude didn't let me finish. "They don't call me anything because they don't know I exist. I do the job, take my money and get the hell out of Dodge before everything goes to hell and people get greedy."

"One of these days one of those guys is gonna talk and rat you out."

"Not a chance. It's generally not a good idea to let criminals know who you are, at least lower-level guys. Works out nicely."

"Nice to meet you Mister Anonymous," I said.

Apropos of nothing, maybe in connection with the word

anonymous, the memory flashed of Jaime looking up into that guy's face and I grimaced. My mind filled in the blanks and then for the hell of it, decided to make up shit that didn't happen, like Jaime kissing the dude, and all at once I just wanted to punch someone. I clenched my fist tight and looked away, fighting down the anger.

Claude seemed to have a sense of what was going on with me. "You gonna be okay, man?"

I thought for a long moment and couldn't get the words out.

Jimmy returned with our drinks, and glad for the distraction, I greedily gulped my whiskey down, enjoying the spreading warmth of the liquid. I put the glass back onto Jimmy's tray and nodded as he handed me a waiting glass of whiskey. I was going to have to remember to make sure Claude tipped him extra.

"Might as well bring four at a time," Claude noted to Jimmy, slipping a hundred dollar bill onto his tray, apparently reading my mind. "I'm going to get a little fucked-up with my friend."

I grinned and raised my glass. Claude raised his glass of water.

"Here's to getting fucked up over a broken heart."

Things got a little blurry after that.

Pro-Tip for Humans #188:
Don't piss off the guy who can make you disappear.

Chapter 8
IT'S A BITTER SWEET SYMPHONY

B *link...*
Boobs. All good bar crawls need to involve boobs at some point. I don't know how I had ended up staring at the faceful of full, round, and perky boobs only inches from my face, but I could only assume it was pure luck on my part. A moment later, a finger under my chin gently but firmly tilted my face upward. I could only smile happily at the owner of the boobs, a very pretty Thai girl with a spray of glitter on her face and a head of platinum blonde hair down to her ass that contrasted sharply with her brown skin. Most likely suicide blonde: dyed by her own hands.

"See something you like?" Suicide Blonde teased and wiggled ever so delightfully in a way that made her boobs boob ever so boobily. She was a tall girl and the backless slinky silver dress was barely enough to contain her boobs. If she raised her arms, there would have been a lot of sideboob on display, and I wasn't complaining.

"I have no idea how I got here, but I am never leaving," I said drunkenly and happily.

"So, do you still miss your ex's boobs?"

"The words, 'not-at-all' come to mind," I lied, the faded memory of Jaime's small and perky boosb flashing across my consciousness. There it was, that pang of longing that came from thinking about Jaime and I tried to shake it off, after all: boobs. In. My. Face.

"You're sweet," Suicide Blonde flirted.

"Harry's going to skin this guy if he catches him in between your boobs like that," a bored sounding voice spoke up behind me. I looked past Suicide Blonde to see who was determined to ruin my enjoyment of such a wonderful and giving paid of boobs. It was a tall leggy brunette who wore a similar dress to Suicide Blone, but she had not been gifted with similar boobage. She stared at her phone, idly flicking through the screens as if to communicate just how bored she was of this entire situation. Her eyes flicked toward me and they were merciless and condescending as fuck.

"Oh lighten up," Suicide Blonde said, "no rules against having fun."

"And just when I thought your standards couldn't get any lower."

I was about to say something pithy and no doubt extremely witty and cutting, but I caught sight of the entire bar for the first time and the words died in my mouth.

The place was huge, almost cavernous with ridiculously high ceilings that somehow still had excellent acoustics for the karaoke singing that was currently in progress. Apparently we were in some kind of karaoke bar that was clearly compensating for something. The enormous stage at the front with the numerous stage lights looked more suited for a huge jazz band than for a singer with a microphone and a monitor. Even with the enormous neon sign that proclaimed "Karaoke at HTDK" (with the HTDK in a rendered logo), it was clear that karaoke wasn't the main business of this club. There was a visibly drunk middle-aged Chinese man on stage, slurring his words through a drunken version of *Sweet Child of Mine*. The striped tie around his forehead made him more idiotic instead of looking like the rebel he had been hoping for.

The bar itself looked like an old factory of some kind that had been converted into a nightclub. The second-floor overhang started at least 30 feet up. It overlooked the entire first floor with a solid floor-to-ceiling wall of thick black glass. It sent the clear signal that upstairs was exclusive as hell, and if you weren't invited, you weren't wanted.

Across the black glass, a projected logo alternated between the HTDK logo and the words *"The Hall of the Drunken King"*.

We were sitting at a low circular glass table in comfortable couches that in turn encircled the table in four rounded sections. Claude sat directly across from me with his arms around two girls who also wore the slinky low-backed shimmery silver dresses that seemed to be the costumes of these particular club girls. They both had long legs that went on for days and sent the signal that they were either very expensive call-girls or models. I don't know why I thought that, okay? They were tall, skinny and I was drunk, so whatever.

Claude and the girls were all laughing, one of the girls wrapping her long fingers through Claude's hair, the other one with her hand on his leg.

"I'm sorry," I mumbled with a glare at Bored Brunette. "What was I saying before? Please tell me it was hilarious."

"You were saying some girl screwed you over," Suicide Blonde murmured and squeezed my leg again, her hand suspiciously higher up my leg.

"So definitely not funny," I sighed. That sounded about right, and this girl, whoever she was just smiled at me.

"Nah, you're sweet," Suicide Blonde said, "I've always been a sucker for sad stories and bad boys."

"Am I the bad boy in this equation?" I gulped.

"You'd better be," she confirmed and in a smooth almost snake-like move, darted her head forward and licked my earlobe.

I definitely had a half-chub at that point and my drunk self was not having a great time realigning itself with reality. Girls like this never found me that interesting and I had the feeling I was about to fumble badly. Had Suicide Blonde told me her name at some point? She *must* have told me, but her name was buried in the fog of drunkenness and the rush of excitement that had made its way to my pants wasn't helping in any way.

Yet, I was having fun, *right*? So much *goddamn fun*.

The drunk Chinese guy moped off the stage to a very scattered and unenthusiastic applause from the handful of people at the bar, and a new singer took the microphone, the opening chords of *Every Rose Has Its Thorn* grabbing my full attention. I glared hatred towards the stage, convinced that the universe was totally fucking with me. Yes, another song from Jaime's playlist. It was like the soundtrack of my life was playing today.

My head throbbed in time with the music, each pulse causing my pickled brain to press against my skull. I wanted to laugh and cry at the same time, scream into the void that was coming for me, *fight back, do anything, anything at all.*

I did the only thing that was logical at the time: I reached out a hand unsteady from the sudden rush of adrenaline and downed my glass of whiskey.

Suicide Blonde squeezed my knee, sending a jolt to adrenaline through my brain. I tore my gaze away from the stupid fucking singer on the stage and directed all of my drunken attention at this gorgeous girl who *wasn't* Jaime. Was she pushing her boobs forward in a way that sent my heart racing again? Why yes she was and they were mesmerizing but--

"Everything reminds me of her," I slurred.

"I want to help you forget her," the blonde said breathily, and biting her bottom lip, leaned in closer to me, all sultry and seductive. I blinked rapidly, confused and then smiled lopsidedly. *Was this chick really that into me? What the hell was going on?*

Bored Brunette watched us in disgust, but then something caught her attention and she mouthed one word, which might have been *"Harry."*

"Time to go, girls," a deep authoritative voice said from behind me. The voice itself wasn't threatening, but it triggered some deep primal urge to *run* and hide and wait for the monster to go away.

It was a weird feeling for me, but it had a different effect on the girls. It was as if someone had flipped a switch. They immediately got to their feet, all friendly smiles now aimed directly at the mystery man. Suicide Blonde smiled crookedly and winked at me as she stepped away with the other girls, no doubt into the arms of Mr Mystery. *Harry,* whoever the fuck he was.

I glanced across the low table at Claude, and he just shrugged nonchalantly, but the signal was there if you knew what to look for: *Cool it, don't make a scene.*

I turned to see who this dude was and understood everything immediately.

The first thing I saw was the pair of brilliant blue eyes that seemed to burn in the dim club interior as if they were able to reach deep into my soul and burn it to a crisp. That primal sense to run was back again, clamouring for attention but I ignored it, mesmerized by the man.

There are certain people you can refer to as "dude", "man", or even "guy." The Middle Eastern man shepherding the girls away from our table was what you could only call "an older gentleman." He didn't look like your average Harry, but once you saw him, the name fit perfectly. He appeared to be in his mid-fifties, but in one glance, I got the sense that he had looked like that *for a very long time,* almost as if he had been born fully-formed. His brown skin contrasted sharply with the strikingly pale blue eyes that seemed to be assessing me with a hard stare and didn't like what they saw. He wore an extremely well-tailored grey suit that had been designed to make people like me feel inadequate just for existing. Whoever this gentleman was, he was dirty rotten filthy stinking rich, and he was dangerous as fuck.

The girls swirled around him, and he tilted his head in our direction as he turned to leave.

"Who the *fuck* are you?" Some drunken idiot slurred. After a second, I realized that the drunken idiot was me.

I was already on my feet, swaying unsteadily. Claude stared at me from across the table, taking the moment to facepalm himself at my stupidity.

Harry slowly turned to look at me again, but for a second, my attention was focused on the women behind him. What struck me in that single moment was the identical looks of terror on their faces. Okay, Bored Brunette looked more amused than anything else, but the other three, they were *terrified* for me, faces pale, eyes darting from me to the gentleman and back again. Suicide Blonde mouthed the word "no," her hands going to her face.

"Leave this place," the gentleman said evenly, no emotion at all.

I meant to stand up for myself, say something quippy that would have ended up with me getting punched, but that didn't happen, no—

Blink...

I found myself outside on the sidewalk, staring at the huge, old and iron-bound wooden doors that led into the club. I had no recollection of how I had gotten there, and since there were no burly bouncers hoisting me into the air by my arms, nor was I face down in the gutter, I must have brought myself outside.

Holy fucking shit! Had I actually just listened to that dude and walked myself out of the goddamn place?

In drunken defiance, I took a step toward the doors—

I found myself turning away, deciding that it wasn't worth my time anyway, and maybe I should just wait out here for Claude—*and what the fuck had just happened?*

Claude strolled out a minute later, looking as suave as fuck. In his suit and crisp white shirt, he wasn't rocking the same disheveled, drunken, day-drinker vibe I was. He had both of our coats draped over one arm.

"Well, that was interesting," Claude noted as he passed my coat to me and I shrugged it on. "You just pissed off Harry De Biers the third and you're still in possession of all your limbs."

"It was time to leave anyway," I mumbled. Then: "Who the fuck is Harry Beers the whatever?"

"Very, very rich. Possible mob-boss depending on who you ask."

"Never heard of him," I said, indignant.

Claude looked at me levelly and seriously. "And *that* is exactly why you should be fucking *terrified* of a man like him."

I glared at the bar. I didn't want to be there anyway, so whatever.

"Fuck this place," I said, and I actually meant it. I had no intention of ever stepping back inside that stupid club ever again. I perked up. "So, where to next?"

Blink...

We were in Claude's condo, or at least I think it was his condo. He moved house every few months, and I hadn't seen his new place since there were weeks that would go by without us actually seeing each other. We had the kind of relationship where time didn't matter and we could pick up in the middle of a conversation as if we had been talking just minutes before. It had amazed Jaime to no end that we never actually said hello or goodbye to each other. Our friendship wasn't based on seeing each other every day: it went far beyond that, so no, I hadn't seen his new place yet.

It was definitely a condo though, and Claude was in the kitchen banging around with pots and pans, making a general ruckus which honestly seemed designed to wake me up. Fucker. He was way too comfortable in the space, so it had to be his condo, right? It would be extremely stupid to take me to somebody else's condo, the state I was in.

I felt the pressure of the firm couch cushion under my butt and squeezed with my hand, feeling the tight, expensive leather. I slumped forward, but that wasn't comfortable, then decided to try sitting. When that didn't work, I slowly laid back, decided that maybe that was not such a great idea since somebody had decided to install a *stupid spinning ceiling.* I sat back up, muscles turning to jelly and just so fucking *useless.* The ceiling, of course, decided to *change direction at that moment,* and that was the thing that just fucked with my head even more. There was the taste of bile at the back of my throat that I tried to swallow and tried to ignore, but I knew what that taste meant, and I was already on my feet, staggering on jellied legs toward what I hoped was the bathroom.

My instincts were right, so of course, I made it just in time. I have a Masters's degree in getting fucked up and prided myself on never having puked on myself or in the back of anyone's car.

There was no fucking way I was going to be throwing up like some punk all over Claude's living room.

"You okay?" Claude called from the other room, and I thought to answer, but ended up puking again, my stomach heaving and clenching as it emptied the contents into the toilet bowl while I hung on for dear life.

Fuck! I hated how that felt.

I somehow made it to my feet again, stomach empty, brow sweaty and clammy, aware that I could hear Claude rummaging around for something.

"You know what sucks?" I asked as I walked back into the living room. "It's that I can't even hate Jaime. None of this is her fault. It's all me."

"Didn't we do this six months ago?"

"It's different this time. Last time, she just dumped me. I could deal with that, you know? This time, she's fucking moved on. It's like we meant nothing, like I meant nothing to her."

"You know that isn't true, right?"

"My head knows it isn't true, but my heart is a selfish asshole, okay?" I collapsed onto the uncomfortable couch, and the room failed to spin this time.

Claude shrugged. "Look: you need to get some sleep. You're fucking drunk, and Louise wants you to meet her tonight at Cecil's. Plus if you don't show up for work, Sammy is going murder you and then come looking for me."

"Work can kiss my ass," I sighed. I turned my head to look at Claude but he had vanished. "Is Louise really coming out? I haven't seen Louise in ages."

"Get some fucking sleep, man."

Something clicked and there was a hum as something mechanical came to life. The room slowly darkened as thick shades lowered over the window, cutting off all of the offensive sunlight. I didn't know it at the time, but it would be the last direct sunlight I would be looking at.

"Did you just do that?" I called out. "Tell me you just did that, becasue it's tripping me the fuck out man."

"Go to sleep Bob," Claude called from far away, his voice echoing in the space.

"You know the one problem with this place?" I called out after a moment.

No answer from Claude.

I sighed deeply and provided the answer for myself: "Not a single boob in sight."

Black.

Pro-Tip for Humans #590:
There's love at first sight, and then there's LUST at first sight.

Chapter 9
DRUNKEN SHENANIGANS AND FORMIDABLE THIGHS

The MILF standing at the bar had not been in anybody's plans, least of all mine.

I strutted into Cecil's Pub like it was my living room, where a massive party was being thrown in my honor. My arrival was almost perfectly timed to the throes of Bush's *"Machinehead,"* which started playing the instant I opened the door. That was the moment I knew the Universe was fucking with me and providing a soundtrack for my life since this was yet another song from Jaime's Infinite Playlist. Still it *was* a bitching playlist. I was still buzzed enough from the day of drinking to not give a fuck if I was being teased or not; besides, I was really looking forward to seeing Louise. Overall I felt pretty damned good.

The aforementioned MILF caught my full attention immediately. With perfect full curves and long legs, she was a snack in a short blue dress and damn: that ass! She noticed me noticing her and noticed me right back, a smile making its way to to her lips as she gave me the best goddamn bedroom eyes I had ever experienced.

Instant woody time.

Holy shit, she's fucking hot, was what I thought.

"Oh, hi there," was what I said as smoothly as possible.

"Hi, yourself," she replied, biting her bottom lip seductively and thoughtfully as she checked me out, and for one heartstopping moment that could have gone sideways, she paid particular attention to the bulge in my pants. She apparently liked what she saw and raised an eyebrow that sent a message my brain interpreted as *yes, she was definitely going to be fucking me tonight.*

I felt a pleasurable rush of endorphins and broke into a goofy grin.

In case you're somehow out of the loop, MILF stands for *Mom I'd Like to Fuck* and had become shorthand for hot older women, in both the porn industry and real life. You can thank the *American Pie* movies for that. Most women didn't even have to be *actual* moms in order to qualify, and in porn it gets particularly confusing. Sometimes women in their thirties who were not moms at all, got lumped into the MILF category just because they were attractive "older women" to the target audience of young males. But wait: what about cougars you ask? Technically, hot older women were called cougars, but only if they had a liking for younger men, but we guys are lazy bastards and the term MILF and cougar had become interchangeable. Go figure, right?

This MILF was an attractive Italian-looking woman with dark shoulder-length hair, late thirties or early forties, but these days who can really tell? She was shorter than me but not by much and had the kind of body that showed the clear difference between a girl and a *woman*. Two other women were with her, a blonde in her forties and a dark-skinned black woman of indeterminate age, neither of whom had noticed me yet, which was probably a good thing. That way they wouldn't be able to convince their friend that I was a bad idea.

Speaking of friends—

Claude grabbed me by the shoulders and gave his most **charming** grin as he turned me around back on track. "I'm sorry, but he's going to have to borrow my friend. We're already late to meet someone he hasn't seen in ages. Right, Bob?"

Claude pointed me into the dining and pool table area where

I spotted Louise, my new 'babysitter.' She sat at a table with a glammed-up Sammy, and upon seeing me, jumped up and sped across the room, a wide grin across her beautiful face.

"Louise!" I practically yelled, breaking free from Claude's grip, leaving him without a drunk friend to redirect.

"And there he goes..." I heard Claude say to no one in particular as I rushed away, lustful temptation pushed to the back of my mind for the moment by the excitement of seeing my friend.

Louise and I ran across the large dining room toward one another like two besotted idiots in a romantic comedy. About halfway, she pretended that she was running in slow motion, so of course I pretended I was running in slow motion, matching her goofiness beat-for-beat. This happened to be right between the two pool tables, and the casually-hip players had to pause for a moment to make sure we weren't going to ruin their masterful display of failure at playing a proper game. Louise and I collided into a slow motion embrace that ended with me wrapping my arms around her and just to close out the metaphor, I swept her off her feet in a romance comedy-worthy spin.

"My god!" she exclaimed as she hugged me back. "How long has it been? Two...? Three...?"

"At least *four* days!" I said dramatically. This was more for the blatant absurdity of it since we hadn't actually seen each other for about two months. We had talked on the phone and Skyped once (or as Microsoft insists that we refer to it *"we video-conferenced using the Skype app"*). Louise worked nights as a doctor in the ER, and I worked graveyard at the porn shop, and for some reason it turned out to be damned hard for our schedules to align. If I ever did, it would usually be just after dark before her shift started, but sometimes even that proved impossible.

Louise had one of those pixie cuts that only look good on certain people, and surprise: she was one of them. She was a few inches shorter than me, so she had to look up to both me and Claude, but she always seemed much taller. Whenever I described her, I would say she was around my height and then be surprised by her real height. Same thing with her eyes: I swore they were dark brown, but then I'd look closer and be stunned that her irises were a pale blue that seemed to glow. Eyes like that you never forget, and yet, somehow I *always* did. Weird right? I used to think that she had a kind of timeless beauty, like someone from a Hollywood depiction of the roaring twenties, which I know is weird, but you'd have to meet Louise to understand what I mean. The words *"like a person out of time"* clamoured for attention, but I pushed them away gently. This was *just Louise,* after all.

Look, what I'm trying to say here is that Louise was *fucking cool.* She was one of the coolest people I had ever met, made cooler by the fact that she had been the one who introduced me to Jaime. Plus, her level of goofiness matched mine, and friends like that you have no choice but to love with all your heart.

"And to think Louise had just managed to convince me she was normal and nothing like you weirdos," Sammy drawled in a way that I could tell she was rolling her eyes. She made her way over, beer bottle in hand.

Louise turned to give her a stunning smile. "Oh, you know you want in on this!"

"Hard pass!" Sammy glowered.

"She's just here to witness my rapid descent into absolute drunkenness," I told Louise, and Sammy grinned evilly.

"What can I say? I love a good trainwreck," Sammy admitted. She nodded in greeting as Claude came over. "Blame Claude, he's the one who mentioned drunken shenanigans, and I'm always down for that."

"Just how drunk *are* you?" Louise asked good-naturedly. "You can still walk and make sentences, so my guess is not quite drunk enough?"

"Somewhere north of being completely 'sloshed', as you like to say," I admitted happily, then added in a stage whisper, "Claude is the worst drinking buddy ever—"

"—And we've reached the part where I go back and tell the bartender to cancel the tab—" Claude threatened wryly.

"What I meant to say is, that he is the absolute *best* drinking buddy in the history of ever!" I corrected myself without missing a beat.

"So an endless variety of dive bars?" Louise asked as she and Claude hugged for just a few seconds longer than was normal among friends. I glared at the two of them, feeling a stab of jealousy, a bitter taste rushing into my mouth.

"Well, you know me and Bob," Claude said with a mock swagger, not noticing my irritation, "we like to keep it classy."

"Do you really have to leave?" Louise pouted at him, and Claude actually looked conflicted.

I watched the two of them, the easy way Claude and Louise stood with their arms around each other's waists, bodies fitting together so *comfortably,* and yes, jealousy that I didn't have that kind of connection with anyone anymore, knifed me in the stomach over and over again like the relentless and determined bastard that it was. There was a rising lump in my throat that didn't want to be swallowed, a sudden lightheadedness as I looked at them and wanted *that* so badly, to *fit* with another human being as easily as they did. Memory, that old motherfucker, made an appearance and kicked me in the teeth with the realization that *I'd already had that with Jaime, oh and by the way buddy, remember how you fucked that up?*

Louise seemed to realize what was going on with me. Maybe it was the utter despair that had leaked from my emotions onto my face; who knows? She left Claude and embraced me warmly, and I let her. Sammy chose that moment to throw her arms around Claude and looked up at him as adoringly as possible.

"So about that tab ..." Sammy wheedled, pushing Claude toward the main bar.

I focused on Louise's hug, and the stabs of jealousy lessened.

"It's okay, Bob. It's going to be okay," Louise said reassuringly, and I believed her.

"Did you know about this new guy that Jaime is seeing?" I asked her, already knowing the answer.

"Of course I knew about him," she said.

"You could have told me," I accused her.

Louise raised her gaze to meet mine, and it was like she was looking into my soul. Did I mention how *deep and blue* her eyes were? You could almost lose yourself in them, if you were so inclined. I felt a sense of calm. *Louise had only my best interests in mind. She was my friend and would never do anything to hurt me. It was all okay.*

"I didn't tell you about him because it was none of your business, sweetie." Louise said, and after a moment, I nodded in agreement.

"You're right," I conceded, "it was none of my business."

Claude and Sammy returned, drinks in hand. I looked at Claude, the smile coming back to my face, the gloom lifting. *What had I been so fucking sad about anyway? I missed Jaime, but so what?*

I looked around the room and instantly locked eyes with the MILF. At least I think I did; it was hard to tell from across the other side of the bar. Screw it, I was going to think of her as *"Brandi"* until I found out. MILF seemed disrespectful. And don't think that I didn't get the irony that this was actually a *mom I wanted to fuck*, either, okay? Work with me here.

Sammy sidled up to me as the four of us made our way back to the table by some unspoken group consensus. I looked at her suspiciously.

"Shouldn't you be sleeping?" I asked in as accusing a tone as I could.

"Shouldn't *you* be getting sober?" Sammy snapped right back. "Your shift starts in about three hours, and by all calculations, you're going to be fucking drunk."

"I'll be fine," I lied.

"You'll be fucking *fired* if the boss catches you."

"We sell porn for a living Sammy," I said evenly and then what I was saying sank in fully. "Nobody cares if the guy who sells them porn is drunk off his ass."

"Speaking of fucking—" Sammy interjected.

"Except we weren't—" I pointed out.

My gaze wandered back to the MILF, my mind already strategizing an approach at the mention of *"fucking"*.

Sammy grabbed my face and pointed it to where Claude and Louise were getting ready to play darts. They were most definitely getting their flirt on.

"Tell me they're not fucking, and I'm going to call you a goddamn liar." Sammy challenged me with a little more force than her amused expression failed to communicate.

"They're not fucking?" I responded, and I wasn't even fooling myself.

"Good god, look at them," Sammy practically moaned, and I just raised a skeptical eyebrow. She nudged me and continued. "If anybody should be fucking and making terrible porn that I'd totally watch, it should be those two."

Sammy had a point. The way that Claude acted around Louise was different than with those girls back at HTDK. With Louise, he was relaxed and comfortable, the light flirting between them actually *meaningful*. This afternoon with the girls, they had been all over him, and he had just been ... *fitting in or something*. There had been nothing behind it at all, like he had been waiting and *watching* for something, possibly for me to screw up. But now, the grin he had on his face as he teased Louise, looking up at him, with a slight tilt to her head, told a different story.

I glanced back at the bar again, but some drunk-looking guy was making apparently unsuccessful moves on the MILF. Sammy snapped her fingers in front of my face, determined to keep my attention.

"How the fuck have you managed to put up with three years of this sexual tension?" Sammy wanted to know. I blinked rapidly, wondering what she was talking about and then realized she was talking about Claude and Louise, not me and the MILF.

"Oh, this only happens like four times a year!" I protested. "Think about the last time you hung out with me and Claude, or me and Louise. It's like the two of them go out of their way to avoid being in the same room together..."

"And once again there's you triggering my imagination with Claude and Louise in a motel room shagging the ever-loving shit out of each other," Sammy said with a lecherous grin.

"'Shagging'? Seriously?"

"It's what she'd call it. Fucking Brits, am I right?"

"Yeah, I don't think that's ever happened, and can we stop shipping my two best friends together now?"

"Oh, I'm not shipping them. This is *all* about them fucking." Sammy made an obscene gesture, sliding her finger into an O formed with the thumb and forefinger of the other hand.

"Are you sure you're not a dude?"

Sammy hit me with the full force of her heavy-mascaraed sensuality, her dark and sultry bedroom eyes promising sexual delights that would start with her pouty blood-red lips, her tongue flicking gently and seductively over her teeth... yet at the same time, my thoughts suddenly swung back to "Brandi."

"Does any of *this* look like a dude to you?" Sammy breathed sensually at me.

I shook my head instead of saying no, unable to summon the word.

"Thought so," Sammy said, and just like that, she turned off the smoulder and drank deeply from her mug of beer, barely containing her smirk.

"Don't tease the drunken man," I complained, and there I was glancing across the room again to where Brandi leaned against the bar watching me like some kind of predator.

"Don't even think about fucking me," Sammy said glibly as she picked up a chicken wing from the basket, "and you won't have to suffer from severe blueballs brought on a case of never-gonna-happen-itis."

I didn't have the heart to tell her that she wasn't the one I was thinking about fucking. *What the hell was it about Brandi anyway? It was like she had hypnotized me or something.*

Sammy tore into the wing, ripping the flesh from the bone, reminding me and anyone watching how much of a predator she was. *Goddamn Sammy.* I glanced at her and then my eyes slid back to the bar where Brandi picked up her purse and said something to her two friends.

All at once, there it was, a stirring in my pants, as interest in less-dangerous quarry peaked. I watched as she excused herself and, with a glance in my direction, made her way through the dining room towards me. The guys playing pool paused to watch her pass, one of the women shoving the butt of her stick in her partner's hip. Somebody was going to get an earful tonight, and it wasn't me.

"Are you teasing Bob again?" Louise asked as she sauntered over and picked up her mug of beer. Claude followed with a wry smile and a glance at his watch.

"It's my solemn duty to torture this poor bastard, so fuck yeah," Sammy smirked.

"Why do you let her do this to you?"

"I'm a masochist *and* an optimist. Around Sammy, that's just asking for it. *It* being trouble."

"Guys, I really gotta take off. Can't be late for this meeting," Claude said, backing away. "Louise, promise to keep him *somewhat* alive?"

Louise shrugged and grinned. "There's no telling what we're going to get up to," she said and blew a kiss to Claude. Claude twirled his finger in the air as a final goodbye and turned to exit, almost colliding with Brandi. He smoothly stepped past her with barely a look and headed towards the exit.

I watched Brandi, mesmerized by the sway of her hips and the curve of her neck. Louise and Sammy were saying something, no doubt verbally sparring with some witty banter that would have amused me for days, but I didn't care.

Brandi breezed past us, and for just a moment, there was a touch of eye contact with a raised eyebrow, and a slight tilt of the head that was *definitely* an invitation. It was one of those "blink and you miss it" moments, but I had caught it, or at least I hoped I had caught it *and holy shit!*

I turned to watch as she headed down the stairs to the bathroom.

"That is a woman who looks like she's been cheated on and is out to do some revenge fucking of her own," Sammy summarized for me.

"Be nice Sammy," Louise warned.

"That *was* me being nice," Sammy said sweetly. "Fuck, I'd do her."

I stood and gulped down the rest of my drink, making up my mind.

"I think I need to go to the bathroom," I said, and then, heart thumping in my chest, I walked toward the stairs desperately hoping that the invitation had not been a figment of my imagination.

Pro-Tip for Humans #654:
writing these things is hard!

Chapter 9
THE CHAPTER WITH THE SEX

Brandi was waiting for me at the bottom of the stairs.

She slipped back around the corner as I made my way down, my head buzzing with anticipation, dick rock hard in my pants and definitely leading the way. I reached the landing and we locked eyes, a sly smile coming to her lips. She took a step closer, hips cocked just so, boops psyched out for maximum effect.

"You never came back like you promised," she murmured, lips red and so mesmerizing. For some reason, I noticed the sharp points of her incisors and wondered what she tasted like.

"Figured you'd find me," I lied with a casual shrug. I really couldn't take my eyes off her lips and found myself moving closer.

"Did you really?" she asked with a raised eyebrow.

"Nah, I was lying," I admitted. "I'm Bob by the way."

"Don't care," she breathed and pushed herself close to me.

Let me be clear here so we understand each other, okay? This kind of thing does not happen to me. In all of my twenty-nine years of life, the closest I had come to a one-night stand or any kind of sordid sex was with this one girl I had a crush on who was leaving town the next day. We had hooked-up after her going-away party and then the next day she was gone. And that had happened when I was twenty-two.

Like most men my age, I had grown up with Hollywood telling me that I was supposed to be having sex at the age of fourteen and that other kids my age were out there doing it. Yes, some of them actually were, but most of them were lying about it. The default answer when asked if you were a virgin was supposed to be an affirmative "hell no" and then a confident smirk as you made up some stupid story that everyone knew you were lying about. The truth is that I didn't even lose my virginity until I was 18, and even then it wasn't like I was getting laid every night. The only thing that changed was that I had the added confidence that women found sexy, and even then, I still wasn't having that sordid Hollywood-type sex. Having a beautiful, confident and sexy older woman want me so openly and then approach me brazenly was completely out of my comfort range, but, you know what? I went with it as best I could and adapted. I knew all of the moves to this dance, so now I just had to make them work.

We ended up in the women's bathroom, and I fumbled the lock on the door while the MILF tore at my shirt, still kissing me hard every chance she got—

The bathroom was one of those single occupancy deals, just a toilet bowl and a sink, identical to the men's bathroom, but for whatever reason, they had decided that the women's bathroom was going to look nicer than the men's. Someone had applied an art-deco style wallpaper to all of the walls, so there was this weird disconnect when Brandi pulled away from me, and I had a chance to notice.

Brandi pushed me away and raised her eyebrow as she dug into her purse. After a moment, she produced a vial of white powder and wiggled it invitingly.

"Wanna get fucked up?"

Brandi poured a line onto her thumb and forefinger, and snorted the heroin with a flourish. She poured another line and held her hand out for me to partake. I dived right in and hoovered that shit right up my nose, feeling that explosion of instant euphoria doubled with triumph had Claude hadn't been able to keep me away from the drugs after all.

Brandi hiked up her already short dress and peeled off her black lacy Victoria's Secret thong. She flicked them into the air with an easy motion of her foot, and I caught them absentmindedly, watching as she leaned forward against the sink and looked over her shoulder at me.

"Get over here and fuck me," she growled.

I didn't wait for a second invitation.

I had heard people going at it hard in different bathrooms over the years, but never once had I imagined it would be me making the grunts that anyone outside the door would be forced to listen to for the next five minutes. Then I stopped thinking of anyone outside the room while I thrust hard at the backside of that very horny MILF, giving everything I had It was the first sex I had had since Jaime, and I was determined to make it count.

Fuck you Jaime. Fuck you hard.

I held on to Brandi's hips, trying very hard to not get my dick bent from being at the wrong angle and getting the timing wrong, because damn that shit hurts. Brandi gasped and squealed with every thrust, clearly enjoying herself, at times going from grabbing the edge of the sink to beating at the walls. Finally she pushed back and paying attention to her signal, I stepped backward, only for her to turn to face me, reaching for my cock. She pulled me close to her and lifted one leg into the air. She pulled me into her, and it was too much for me. I pushed her back against the sink, one hand hooked around the back of the knee of the raised leg, the other hand grabbing her ass as I pushed deeply into her. She kissed me fiercely, our tongues entangling as we fucked, her light-green eyes intent on my own brown ones, daring me to take her, take all of her. Her nails scraped on my shoulders and back, every moan from her lips in sync with my thrusts.

"I'm cumming!" I managed to gasp, but she didn't push me away, only pulled me closer, her nails digging into my back now, and then I exploded inside her, and she moaned--

Brandi bit down on my neck and I yelped, caught in the moment, pain and pleasure mingling in a confusion of emotion and holy shit that hurts—

I pulled away from her, and all I could see was that her mouth was red with blood. My blood. Her hot pink tongue flicked out of her mouth, licking away the last vestiges of blood on her lips.

"What the fuck is wrong with you?"I fairly spat at her.

She moved away from the sink, pulling down her skirt, and glowered at me. "I like to leave my mark," she said. "Figured a guy like you's gotta be cheating on his girlfriend, and now she knows you've been with me."

"But you fucking bit me!" I protested. "You didn't have to do that!"

"I got caught up in the moment," Brandi admitted. "Just be glad you didn't cum in my mouth." She gnashed her teeth for effect, then wiped her mouth with the back of her hand before pulling open the door.

"Can I get my underwear back?" Brandi asked.

I wadded the underwear up and pressed them against my fresh wound. *Motherfucker! That hurt!*

"I'm keeping these!" I snarled at her.

Brandi wrinkled her nose at me and stuck out her nose at me. The door clicked shut and I just stood there, pants around my ankles, erection slowly fading, my neck throbbing in pain, and wondered what the fuck I was going to do now. The door clicked open after a moment and Bandi poked her head back in.

"Hey, you wanna go again?" Brandi asked.

"No!"

So yeah, that was how I ended up returning to the bar with Brandi's black lacy thong wadded up on my bleeding neck. I had soaked them in water and tried to wash the wound but had given up. Fuck it. I just needed some alcohol and painkillers and I could tough it out.

Louise was waiting for me at the table and it was almost like she sensed me before she saw me. She turned to me and her mouth dropped open.

"What the fuck happened to you?" That was her first shocked question, then a beat later: "Are those panties?"

"It's not that bad," I lied. "Stings a little, but then again it *is* a bite—"

"*She bit you?*" Louise's eyes blazed with fury; she turned, scanning the room for the skanky bitch who had bitten me. "That is the height of *rudeness!*"

"It's just a bite," I tried to play it off, "how bad can it be?"

Louise turned her rage on me.

"You utter idiot! The human mouth utterly filthy!" She snatched the panties away to examine my neck, then with a grimace, turned me around so she could get a better look, talking all the while. "There are up to a thousand different kinds of bacteria present in your mouth at a time. I once treated a patient for hepatitis B *and* C after he made the mistake of breaking his fist on some other idiot's teeth. He also had to get a tetanus shot and believe me, those are never fun." A sharp pain shot through my shoulder and I hissed in pain. "If dogs weren't in the habit of licking their own asses so much, their mouths might be said to be cleaner than ours. We do not take bites lightly and believe me, we see a lot of bites."

Louise stopped her examination and I turned to face her, my shoulder and neck throbbing. Smething trickled down my back and after moment I realised that I was bleeding.

"It's not like she had rabies," I joked and only earned a withering glare from Louise as she dialed a number on her phone.

"If rabies was the only thing that skank had, you can count yourself lucky," Louise hissed at me. "Please tell me that used a condom?"

I gave a thumbs up and a hopeful grin.

"Whoa, what the fuck happened to you?" Sammy aked from behind me. I half-turned to look at her, but even that was difficult and painful.

"Idiot let that skank bite him," Louise said, distracted with her phone.

"I did not let anybody bite me!" I protested.

Sammy failed to look even a tiny bit empathetic.

"Well *that* sounds like a fun story that you're going to have to tell me later," Sammy said and downed the rest of her drink. "My Uber is here in two minutes, so peace out bitches!"

Sammy deliberately punched me on the shoulder and I winced as pain shot through my neck and shoulder. Sammy gave Louise a half-hug and smacked playfully on the ass as she exited.

"Your friends are cooler than you Bob!" Sammy called out a final insult as she exited. I gave her a half-hearted middle-finger as a reply, but my heart wasn't in it. Why was my shoulder hurting so much now? *Fuck!*

Louise swore and typed rapidly at her phone.

"How are you holding up?"

"Pain. Hurt. Ow. Like that."

"We have to get you disinfected and maybe some stitcheec," Louise noted. She read her phone and nodded in triumph. "Luckily, I have a friend who is a nurse, and he lives about four blocks from here. He should have exactly what we need so we can get you patched up there."

"Wicked," I murmured.

Louise scanned the room again, lips pursed.

"And then I'm going to come back and kick that bitch's *ass.*"

Pro-Tip for Humans #69:
Never trust a man that says "trust me." Trust me on this.

Chapter 10
THE BEAUTIFUL PEOPLE

I tried not to scream every time Louise drove her Honda over a bump or into a pothole, but she wasn't making it easy. She winced and apologized as she went over each bump and I hissed or yelped in response, but apologies were no help for the throbbing pain in my shoulder and neck. The neighbourhood she had driven us into apparently employed an overzealous road-planner, and that psychopath decided the best idea in the world was to install traffic-bumps every fifty-feet.. Then again, it was a moderately-wealthy neighbourhood so it shared that counter-intuitive characteristic with all wealthy neighbourhoods I'd ever driven through: fantastically shitty roads.

Bump!

"Ow!"

"Sorry!"

Bump!

"Motherfuck!"

"So sorry!"

Bump!

"Rasshole!" I yelled as spasms of pain coursed through my shoulder, forcing out my favourite Bajan cussword, which I had learned from my Dad many years ago. Dad was an expert cusser and I was an apt pupil, soaking them all up to use at the appropriate time. There's nothing like a Bajan cussword to really communicate just how fucked up everything is. A time like *this* one.

My shirt was sticky with blood all the way down my back and creeping into my underwear. I was sure it had soaked through the lining of my coat, and there was a moment of regret since that had been my favorite (and only) wool-coat. I had bled steadily since we left the bar and I was sure that wasn't normal.

Lights from the dashboard illuminated Louise's furrowed brow and slightly panicky eyes. "Here we are," she announced, parking the car in front of one of the older houses in the neighbourhood. "We'll get you fixed up in no time at all, but you have to promise to behave, okay?"

"You promised me heroin," I groaned.

"Vicodin, Bob," Louise disagreed, "and only if you were not showing any improvement."

"No, it was definitely heroin."

Louise held up her phone to show a text message from Claude.

Claude: NO ILLEGAL DRUGS FOR BOB!
Dammit Claude.

"Nice try, buddy." Louise rolled her eyes, retrieved two pills from her pocket, and deposited them into my hand. She reached into the back for something, and I made the pills disappear into my mouth, paused to gather enough saliva and swallowed.

"I had water you know," Louise admonished, holding the bottle of water she had been searching for. She glanced at the house and then back at me. "Look, my friend can be a bit of a dick, but he'll help. Please promise to behave?"

"Me behaving starting… now," I said and winced. Even talking was painful, but hopefully the Vicodin would kick in soon. The heroin I had gotten from Brandi wasn't helping as much I had hoped. I knew from experience that a proper hit should have had me feeling the pain but really not giving a shit. Good sex but bad drugs.

I somehow managed to exit the car, moving carefully as if I had injured my back, since that was the only movement that seemed to work. Louise watched, ready to lend a hand, but I gave her my best fake grin and waved off her help.

Walking stiffly, I followed Louise down the short driveway to the Victorian-style mansion with the well-kept garden, aware of a distant sound of a house party coming from somewhere. There was a garage at the end of the driveway, a newer and obvious add-on, in front of which a number of cars were parked, including a Black BMW with dark tinted windows, stylishly cool. It spoke volumes about the owner, saying that he was coolly efficient, confident and just rich enough to think that he was ten-times better than you, and that he didn't obsess over cars. If you were richer than he was, then it wouldn't faze him one way or the other, *dammit*. He probably walked around the house in a cardigan or something equally as metrosexual.

Louise banged on the door a couple of times, and after a moment, a ridiculously handsome man opened the door. He wore an elaborate silk robe, loosely belted at the waist, exposing a torso that would have looked at home on the cover of a romance novel. There was a pair of rockstar sunglasses on his face, and when he popped them down to get a better look at me, I noticed that he had the same brilliant pale blue eyes as Louise.

"This the guy?" he asked Louise, waving dismissively at me.

"Robert," Louise said in greeting, "this is Bob, and he needs some medical attention, like *I said on the phone*. He went and got himself bit, but he's been drinking all day, so of course he's not clotting."

"He got bit by a *human*?" he asked, taken aback. For some reason his use of the word "human" instead of "person" was a little unnerving.

I felt I had to defend myself. "Risky bathroom sex," I said off-handedly and more than a little bit cocky. Robert didn't look like the kind of guy to engage in risky *anything*, so I felt like I had the advantage of him on that score.

"A skank bit him," Louise interjected.

"I'd high-five you, but I really don't want to," Robert said. I somehow resisted giving him the double-middle-finger salute, but only just barely. Robert gave Louise an appraising look. "I was actually hoping that you were using this as an excuse for some risky sex of your own."

Louise ignored my shocked expression. "Hard pass Robert."

"Well, damn," Robert shook his head ruefully. "Emergency room is about four kilometres that way."

"Oh come on, pal," I tried on my best grin, "help out a fellow Bob."

That seemed to amuse him, the corners of his lips twitching into a hesitant smile.

"At least he's funny," Robert muttered, and then looked around as if someone might be watching before throwing the door wide open for us to enter. The *THUMP THUMP THUMP* of club music bass pulsed out at us, the universal sign that Robert had one hell of a house party in progress. "Fine, you can come in,"he grumped at us, "but this is one of the worst nights you could be stopping by."

I stepped past Robert into a darkened room with swirling party lights that pulsed in time with the music. Shadowy figures of two naked women danced to the music in the next room and I had to look again to make sure that my mind wasn't fucking with me. Yes those silhouetted boobs were *definitely* naked.

There was a pair of legs in the air, and I turned to see the naked figure of a man with his ass pumping away at a woman on the couch. A woman and two men watched from the sidelines, faces hidden in shadow. I turned slowly and there was a pair of men at the dining table, red strobe lights dancing across their entangled bodies. Three naked women wearing nothing but pearl necklaces exited the room and made their way up the stairs.

Holy shit! Louise brought me to an orgy! Robert's mention of risky sex suddenly made complete sense. And there I was, all proud of my risky bathrrom sex like an amateur.

I turned back to whisper this remarkable fact to Louise, but from the look on her face, she already knew, and she was regretting her decision.

I said it anyway. "Hey Louise!" I hissed gleefully. "This is an orgy!"

"You promised to behave!" Louise glared at me.

"I am being-haved! But in all fairness, we made that deal

before I knew *we were coming to an orgy!*"

Louise stepped forward fiercely and looked me deep in the eye. "Robert Alfredo Manuelo Adolphus Diego, you *will* be on your best behaviour."

I gave Louise my loopiest smile and bopped her on the nose with my finger. "No! And You can't make me!"

Robert leaned forward and whispered into Louise's ear. "He's pretty stoned. You know it doesn't work when they're stoned."

I had no idea what that meant, and the thought occurred to me to ask, but then the thought also occurred that I didn't care. *We were at an orgy dammit!*

Louise very deliberately reached out and poked me in the shoulder. I screamed, while trying *not* to scream. I failed badly but impressively.

"Robert, be a love and take us to a room where I can help my idiot friend," Louise said, as I reeled about the hallway in equal amounts of pain, surprise and betrayal.

"You used to be fun, Louise" Robert sighed. "Hey, Bob-man, think you can manage to not stare so much at my guests? You're ruining the vibe, man."

I nodded, tears streaming down my face. The naked people fucking around me was the last thing on my mind at that very moment, but whatever, right?

I made momentary eye contact with a stunningly-attractive tall blonde woman who was bent over a table, moaning loudly, a well-muscled man pounding her from behind with an extreme effort. The woman winked at me as she ran her tongue over her teeth, and I couldn't help but notice how pointed and sharp-looking her incisors were. Of all of the things I could notice about a woman getting fucked not two feet from me, and I was looking at her teeth, but that's heroin for you.

The thing that really got me though, was the colour of her *eyes*. They were the same shade as Louise's, almost luminescent in the dark.

Funky.

A skinny naked Indian man with a huge cock passed by and glanced at me. Once again, and in stunning contrast to his brown skin, there were the *blue eyes* again. Those blue eyes were everywhere I turned, same blue eyes, different faces. Two women going down on a tanned guy in a corner: blue eyes. The tall leggy brunette who aggressively rode some dude's face to orgasm, hands roughly grabbing his hair: blue eyes. I felt the Vicodin finally kicking but wondered if Brandi's heroin wasn't stronger than I had initially thought, because this shit was tripping me out.

What. The. Fuck?

"Follow me," Robert said, walking past me, further into the house. Louise gently laid a hand on my shoulder and guided me after him.

"Sorry about that," Louise whispered. "I need you to focus on getting that bite cleaned up. I really don't like how much blood you're losing, so just work with me, and we can get through this, okay?"

The words sank in and I thought carefully about what everything really meant, but the effect of the drugs was making thinking a little difficult. I chased a thought, tried to form a sentence or even a word, then finally gave up and presented Louise with a very enthusiastic thumbs up.

"You are way more stoned that you should be," Louise observed.

"Yes, I am," I agreed happily.

We followed Robert, descending into the bowels of the house, the heavy club music fading as we walked further down the stairs. The sound isolation in the house was amazing to witness, going from the main floor to the basement

"So you want to tell me what we're working with?" Robert asked as he unlocked a door at the bottom of the stairs.

"Human bite on the upper trapezius. Possible puncture to the exterior jugular. He's been keeping pressure on it, but we've got a steady flow with no clotting so... yeah: not happy."

We entered what looked like a cross between a tattoo parlour and a very comfortable dentist's office. The floor was all white tile, the walls a dark polished wood with a mixture of expensive looking artwork, obvious by the hideously gaudy frames designed to grab attention. Claude could possibly have identified some of the pieces, but of course I was utterly clueless, despite two years of art history. Admittedly I had spent most of that time studying the lines, shape, and textures of a girl named Christine more than those of Klimt or Carravagio.

"Whoa," I said instead and Robert just shrugged like it was no big deal.

Louise turned to take my coat and frowned when she got a good look at how much blood had soaked into my shirt. Robert made himself busy pulling out scary supplies from the cabinets along the walls.

"You're going to have to help me get my shirt off," I lamented. "I think it's stuck to me."

We spent a few minutes with me turning in circles and trying to wiggle out of the shirt while Louise chased me to make me stop spinning. Once I stopped moving and cooperated, she used a huge pair of scissors to cut the shirt away and then proceeded to peel the fabric from me. It got a little stuck around the wound and the wadded up paper towels that we had used to apply pressure as a replacement for Brandi's thong, but we managed.

"I thought you said you only gave him Vicodin," Robert observed.

I put my finger to my lips. "Shh! I had some heroin earlier," I whispered very loudly. "*Don't tell Louise.*"

Robert was very amused.

"I won't tell Louise a thing," Robert agreed with a sly wink at Louise. "She's no fun."

There was a fancy-looking medical chair in the center of the room, which I gladly climbed onto and tried to make myself comfortable on the cold leather. Or at least tried to. There were no handles on the chair, so I had to fold my hands onto my lap, but then my arm would begin to slide down and because there was no arm to the chair, it would just dangle awkwardly, so I'd have to put it back into my lap. This went on for a few turns until I realised how stoned I was acting and forced myself to settle down, but damn it wasn't easy, especially since there were no arms on the chair, and *I didn't know where to put my arms dammit.*

I grinned happily at Robert, digging my buzz. I really couldn't help myself. Getting high makes me smile a lot and man, I was fucking high. My shoulder didn't hurt so much anymore, everybody was so fucking nice and so cool, there was a fucking orgy in the fucking house, and my bestest friend in the whole wide world Louise was here with me.

"You're the best friend ever," I burbled to Louise, and she gently patted my hand.

I glanced at Robert, who was efficiently cleaning my shoulder, and I really appreciated just how *cool* he was. He had put on a surgical mask but hadn't bothered with a shirt, so it was quite an odd sight that made me want to laugh. Even how he was sewing me up with that needle, just so fucking *cool*. Like, seriously man, who lets complete strangers into the middle of their orgy like that? And goddamn his eyes were so fucking *blue*.

"I like your eyes," I slurred at him. I looked around and found Louise at the foot of the chair hovering nervously. "I like your eyes too. What the fuck is up with the eyes, can somebody tell me that?"

Louise smiled ruefully. "Contact lenses Bob, nothing else."

"Yeah, right," I challenged her.

"The truth is that we're both vampires," Robert said with a smile in his blue eyes. "All vampires have eyes like this."

"I want eyes like that," I replied thoughtfully. I had a thought, lost it and found another one. "Can I get the eyes *without* the rest of the vampire thing?"

"You don't want these eyes, Bob," Louise said quietly. "They come with so much baggage…"

"Are you and Claude fucking?" I asked and then nearly crossed my eyes trying to look at my mouth. Where the fuck had that even come from?

Louise turned a bright red and threw a quick embarrassed glance at Robert, confirming my suspicions that somebody was having risky sex besides me. Go Louise!

She didn't get a chance to answer. The doors slammed open, and we all turned to look at what the hell was going on. A naked Asian woman had entered and she alternated between hyperventilating and sobbing. She was covered in blood, pert breasts framed perfectly in red, her face sprayed in splashes and dots that made it seem that she had just stepped off the set of a horror movie.

She was freaking the fuck out, but since she was covered in what seemed to be someone else's blood--

"Derek fucking cut Sandy's carotid!" she said shakily. "It's a fucking bloodbath upstairs!"

"She's got red on her," I noted sagely, just in case they had missed it.

Louise and Robert had already started to move from the time the woman had entered, their doctor instincts kicking in hard. Robert grabbed a huge white medical-looking bag from somewhere and ran toward the door, right behind Louise. They barrelled past the blood-covered woman, and I heard Louise yell out.

"*Sebastien!* Stay with my friend! Make sure nothing happens to him!"

I was about to mention to the empty room that Sebastien was a stupid name for a traumatized Asian woman, but then a tall man stepped into the room and that made sense

What *didn't* make sense was that I *knew* the dude. I *knew* that perfectly punchable and handsome face, and that hair that could only be described as lustrous. Of course, he hadn't been naked the last time I had seen him with Jaime looking up at him so adoringly, but I recognized him just the same.

"Oh, hey, I know you," I slurred, and tried to sit up, but my muscles didn't seem to be working properly.

The look of confusion on his face was classic as he tried to figure out if I was full of shit or if he was going to tell me to fuck off.

"This is an orgy. Does Jaime know you're here?" I asked accusingly. A shocked thought made its way across my fucked up mind, and I had to ask. "Is Jaime here?"

Sebastien (if that was really his name) cocked his head, seeming to finally recognize me, and he smiled, but there was nothing pleasant about that smile. It was the smile of a predator who had just found its drugged and fucked-up prey.

"Soon-Yi, go get cleaned up," he said to the woman who had finally settled on desperately sobbing, and she nodded gratefully. "I'll stay here with our guest."

He waited until she had left the room before he turned back to me and smiled again. I tried again to get up and failed miserably.

"The fuck is wrong with me?" I asked, but it sounded like I couldn't even form my words anymore.

"I didn't recognize you at first," Sebastien admitted as he stalked ever closer. "Bob. Or as Jaime refers to you: 'that bastard Bob.' Catchy, right?"

"Jaime talks about me?" I almost smiled.

There was a moment of silence where Sebastian and I regarded each other, then he smirked.

"Have you ever had one of those fantasies about beating up the guy who fucked up your girlfriend's life? Come on, you can tell me if you have. We've all thought about it at times, you know? Especially when you meet some truly wonderful girl who totally gets you, but then you discover that there's an *asshole* boyfriend in her past who left her with scars. Usually emotional scars, but every now and again there are literal scars. So you concoct a fantasy where you get to enact the perfect revenge on that *asshole* and you get to be the fucking hero. You tell yourself it's because you can't bear the thought of someone hurting your girl, but in truth, it's because you wanted to be the first to hurt her, but you'll never admit it." He paused, looking at the tray of tools in front of him. After a moment he smiled even more humorlessly. "Except that never happens. Ever. It's just a fantasy after all. The most that would happen is you'd get arrested for assault or whatever, and you'd just be another asshole in a long line of assholes." He smiled, and when he raised his hand in surprised surrender, one of them was holding a scalpel. "And yet, here we are. You, the asshole junkie ex-boyfriend, and me… the guy who's going to kill you."

"*Fuck you buddy,*" I managed to groan. Fucking asshole was all talk-

His hand flicked out almost delicately, and I almost laughed to mock him, but there was a rush of warm wetness down my neck and arm, a flood of liquid where none should have been.

Sebastien stepped back, but I didn't care about him. I tried to clamp a hand onto my neck, finding the strength from somewhere, but even that was useless, and I fell off the chair, not even feeling the pain of my face meeting the floor, only seeing all of the thick red blood that was spreading rapidly across the white tiles.

My blood.

I would have laughed if I could have. Instead, I weakly turned to look at my murderer. If I was going to die, I would go out like I had lived my life.

I raised both middle fingers and flipped that motherfucker off.

Black.

Pro-Tip for Humans #100:
you spend your entire life not dying.

Chapter 12
LIFE, DEATH & EVERYTHING IN BETWEEN

blood

   pain

      touch

         drifting
         is that a voice?

i hate my life.

There are voices in the fog, arguing, yelling even, and I know one of them, knew one of them, but that seems so long ago, another lifetime that happened to someone else, someone who isn't so goddamn cold. Someone who isn't me.

blood

   pain

      touch

         drifting
         did someone speak?

what is life?

This time different voices. Someone punches me in the chest, and I want to tell them not to do that, that is a chest that belongs to me, but it occurs to me that I have no voice. The dead have no mouths, and that's what I'm supposed to be. Dead. Then the thought occurs that if I'm dead, why does it hurt so much? Or is that the memory of pain? And on the subject of pain, is *it supposed to hurt this much? My veins burn liquid fire, my muscles screaming, and I want to scream or laugh or cry but this is a memory. Or is this even happening?*

This had better not be a dream sequence. I hate *dream sequences.*

blood

       pain

           touch

               drifting

           is that a voice?

i hate my life.

The taste of blood fills my mouth. It is not like when you bite your lip or your tongue, and there is that bitter taste of copper like when you lick the contact points on a 9-volt battery. If you grew up with a healthy fear of electricity and don't know what I mean, you're missing out. This taste is sharper, fuller, more alive if that makes any sense at all. It is more like someone has filled my mouth with blood until it is pouring out of my mouth. The taste is everywhere, it encompasses my entire being—

—and goddam

           it

                    is

                              good.

blood

"—not gonna be here when he wakes up," someone says. I struggle to attach a face, a name, a person to the someone. Louise. She doesn't sound like her normal self. It's like she's freaking the fuck out. "They're going to be coming for me."

I can't open my eyes. She is just one of the voices in the fog. There is another one, a woman, further away. She has the kind of voice that sounds like she's always doing something else more important, and this clearly isn't it.

"Let them come," the woman says. "You can fight them. We'll fight them together."

"Harry's let them off their leashes while you've been away," Louise replied. "They're worse now. They changed. You went away and everything changed. A lot of good and a lot of bad, and then... there's them. The Gentlemen."

"Let them come after me then," the other one says. "I haven't had a decent fight in forever. I could do with some random acts of violence. Or focused acts of rage. Same to me either way. Maybe we can make the Seven O'Clock News!"

"Why are you doing this?" Louise asks after a moment.

"Because you needed me," the woman says softly. "Because you asked me."

Either the conversation grows indistinct or I'm drifting off. It feels like they're a hundred feet away, and I'm underwater, struggling to hear. It feels like I'm drowning and there's nothing I can do about it.

I close my eyes.

And then I close them again.

pain

It is a shitty motel room, the kind that you can rent by the hour. It smells like sweat, ass, and musty liners, the kind that you don't want to inspect too closely. It is the kind of room where turning on a blacklight would reveal more stains on the wall than actual wall and makes you want to turn it right back off again.

I have been in cheap shitty motel rooms before, but nothing like this. It is like a hostel that has been taken over by homeless people who then used all of the available funds to fuel their drug habits before realizing that they at least need to put some kind of furniture into the rooms. So yes, there is a bed, the shittiest bed you can imagine with possibly the shittiest mattresses available. There is a tv, a relic from the nineties, and looks like it had been purchased second-hand from a thrift shop of highly questionable character. The tv sits on top of a black, battered Lack table from Ikea, the kind you can pick up for $15 or $9.99 in the AS-IS section if you get there on a Wednesday morning (they clear the displays on Tuesday nights, so it's prime pickings on Wednesday mornings). A single plastic chair that looks like it would break as soon as you look at it, is the room's only other furniture.

It is the kind of room you wake up in if the gang of idiots you had been partying with the night before, had been too broke to get a proper motel, but not broke enough to sleep it off in an alley and possibly get mugged and arrested.

Louise peers intently out of the room's only window, the light on her face slowly changing from blue to red to blue to red again in time with the unseen flashing neon light somewhere outside. The way she is dressed definitely gives me some weird action movie or violent video game vibes, the type of game where the bad guys have bigger guns and know exactly where you are. When she raises her hand to part the threadbare curtain, I'm not surprised that she is holding a massive black hand-cannon that looks like it came directly out of a Lara Croft movie. Four large black military-looking machine guns lean against the wall next to the tv.

Fucking surreal, right?

To add to the surreal nature of everything, I realize at that moment that I'm lying naked on the middle of the bed. Oh, and there is a spring poking me right in the middle of the ass-cheeks; a couple of inches down, and I'd be referring to the mattress as Dr. Mattress. In case that was too subtle for you: because it would be sticking right up my asshole.

"Is this a dream?" I manage to mumble, and Louise glances back at me, her eyes wide with surprise.

"Unfortunately, this part is all real," Louise says with a half-smile.

"That's what I'd expect a dream to say." I try to sit, and my body gives me the middle finger as my head is taken over by a tribe of tiny invisible pixies with jackhammers and bad attitudes. I don't realize how bad it is until I collapse onto the floor, my legs having been replaced by jello when I wasn't looking.

The room spins

and

reality

snaps

into

place with a resounding—

"Ow."

When I was able to see again, Louise was looking down at me, her brilliant blue eyes wide with concern.

"I think I need more drugs,"

"I'm not sure that this carpet has ever been cleaned, but the good news is that you won't have to worry about contracting any horrible diseases from it, so there's that."

Through my pounding headache with one persistent jackhammer pixie refusing to get off the back of my head, I struggled to make sense of what she was saying. I rose very, very slowly, ignoring Louise's offered hand of assistance, and the room didn't spin so much **this time**.

"That must have been one hell of a party," I groaned. A memory flashed across my mind looking for someplace to settle, but the jackhammer pixie wasn't having any of it.

"Yeah, about that," Louise said in a way that was so obviously loaded that it got my immediate attention. "Normally, I would have more time to do this and ease you into it, but time is of the essence, so I'm just going to break it to you and get it over with."

The bottom dropped out of my stomach and I looked at Louise in shock, suddenly very self-conscious of how naked I was. *Holy fucking shitballs—*

"We didn't have sex did we? *Is that why I'm naked?*"

Louise's raised eyebrow and exasperated sigh told me everything I needed to know about that possibility and calmed my fluttering heart.

"No, you doorknob: we didn't have sex."

"Well that's a relief."

"You died last night, and I had to turn you into a vampire in order to save your life."

She waited for my reaction, and I just nodded, waiting for more. Then to break the silence—

"Okay, cool. Is that all?"

"Seriously? I tell you that I turned you into a vampire, and that's your response?."

"Oh, I'm assuming that this is still part of the dream sequence. I was waiting for the scene to change but nothing is happening yet." I looked around the suspiciously non-dreamlike room.

It occurred to me that this was the first time I had ever had a headache in a dream. "Man, this is one fucked up dream," I observed.

Louise pinched the bridge of her nose and began to pace, head bowed, eyes squeezed shut.

"What are you doing?" I finally asked.

"Counting to twenty," Louise responded without missing a step, "and trying very hard to remember why I saved your life."

"Oh that one is easy! Because I'm awesome!"

Lousie paused, sighed, and walked over to the window. She gestured for me to join her. I grabbed a sheet from the bed and wrapped it around me to make a rudimentary and mildew-scented toga. I looked like an actor with a no-nudity clause in a move that had no budget for nicer sheets, but at least my junk wasn't swinging in the breeze.

My legs had congealed into something with a bit more substance— more rubber than jello — so I was able to deny the reintroduction to the floor that gravity insisted would be good for me, but my stomach had decided to join in on the "let's fuck up Bob" festivities. It was like there was a fist clenching my stomach, and it squeezed hard three times, and then released, waited for a bit and then repeated.

I was beginning not to like this dream. At all.

I joined Louise at the window and winced as I squeezed out a fart, praying that it would be silent and not smelly, and that was all my stomach needed to chill the fuck out.

"Sorry," I whispered.

Louise looked out the window, and I looked with her. The window looked out onto a short alley that led to what looked like King Street East and Spadina Avenue. I actually recognized the Sushi restaurant across the street, so that placed us right in the heart of downtown.

"You're about to go through some changes in your body, and it's going to hurt a lot. Your genetic structure is rewriting itself, rewiring how your body deals with trauma, how you smell, feel... everything. Everything is going to taste *amazing* and that's good *and* bad, but I swear it's one of the best things. This is what vampirism does. It throws out all the inconvenient bits and makes you better, but it hurts like a sonofabitch. You're going to feel like you're dying, and there are times when you will wish you could die, but it will pass, and you will get through this."

"You sound like you're saying goodbye," I noted.

"I so wish I could be there for you when you've gone through the change, but what I did was against the rules, and the guy in charge is a massive prick who doesn't like people breaking his goddam precious rules. So he's sent some very bad men for me, and from what I've heard, nobody ever survives a visit from them."

As if on cue, a slim elegant figure stepped into the mouth of the alley and raised his head slightly to look up at the window. It was as if he could see us and he wanted us to know. An actual chill ran down my spine, this rippling of *fear,* a sudden rush of adrenaline like I had never experienced. The base of my spine went ice cold as if someone had shoved a block of ice back there, and sweat beaded on my forehead at the same time. Heat rose from my upper lip, almost like a physical presence and it was almost as if I could *inhale* it, could taste it, the smell of my *own fear.*

I recoiled forcefully, stepping back away from the window, panic rising in me, desperate for that monster in the shape of a man not to see me.

"Holy fuck—"

Louise glanced out the window and nodded with a deep sigh.

"That's Mister Flynn. The other two will be along shortly, but he's the most dangerous one."

"There's three of them?" I dared a look again, and sure enough there were three men now. The slim one Louise had referred to as Mr. Flynn was in the middle, flanked on one side by an imposible giant of a man and on the other, a skinny one —erratic and twitchy and in constant motion.

All doubt concerning the existence of monsters, evaporated at the sight of those three in the alleyway. Those three—

"What the fuck are they?" I hissed in terror.

"They're *vampires,* Bob. Have you not been listening?"

"Vampires don't exist!"

"I'll stay here while you go out and explain that to them."

"Hard pass—" I interrupted myself with a loud and long belch that seemed to go on forever. It was a long *braaaaaaaaaaaaaap* that left my throat burning, and my mouth tasting like the liquid from the bottom of a dumpster. It left me bent over and gagging, struggling to stay upright on trembling legs.

Louise holstered her pistol and picked up one of the machine guns for a final inspection, hands moving quickly in a well-practiced rhythm. I think that's when I realized I might not be asleep. And if this was reality, I was totally fucked. The Louise I knew was a caring and compassionate person, a doctor who was passionate about working in the Emergency Room where she could do the most good. That woman was the one who had let me stay with her for three months after I had been kicked out of my old apartment after being laid off from the internet start-up. That Louise was the person who had (inadvertently) introduced me to her best friend in the world, a woman named Jaime, and had been happy that we had seemed made for each other.

This Louise was apparently a body-armor-wearing weapons expert, who was ready to fight three bona-fide terrifying monsters.

This Louise was a motherfucking *vampire*.

Please fasten your seatbelt: up is now down, left is right, and by the way, gravity still sucks.

"We call them the Gentlemen. Even other vampires are terrified of them, because what they do is, well... they kill other vampires."

"I want to wake up now Louise," I pleaded through a desperate not-grin, my mind teetering on the edge of terror and insanity. *"Please let me wake up!"*

"Still not a dream Bob," Louise said as she checked the magazine on another gun. "I'm a vampire, and in three days, your change is going to be over, and you'll be one too. A vampire just like me. But only if I can get these walking slabs of evil away from you."

My stomach cramped suddenly, and a wet-sounding fart exploded out of my ass before I could even try to control it. What is widely known as a "shart" and in the worst cases will leave a spray of wet shit inside your underwear. Totally gross. A vile and obnoxious odour immediately took over the room, and both Louise and I gagged. Louise reeled away, trying to escape.

"Oh, gods! It got into my mouth!"

"Serves you right for turning me into a vampire," I quipped and then gagged again. "Good god that's terrible."

"It's the change. I'd forgotten how bad it is." Louise spat and covered her mouth and nose with the arm of her armoured jacket.

Not wanting to move too much in case another *shart* caught me by surprise, I glanced at the window and then back at Louise.

"So I died?" I was surprised to find myself asking. My stomach gurgled at me, right before my stomach clenched again, hard this time. I was surprised to find sweat pouring off my body like I was in a sauna. On the plus side, the jackhammer pixie was apparently on lunch break, leaving only a cold spike of pain right between my eyes that made it incredibly hard to focus.

"Why did you turn me?" I found myself asking. "Why did you save me? Doesn't this go against the doctor's oath or something?"

Louise looked at me like I was the stupidest person on earth.

"Because you're my friend, and I love you, dummy," she said. She shouldered the rifle and grinned crookedly, looking like the total badass that she was. "Stay here. I'm going to go and make some noise. I'm really hoping these guys haven't learned how to dodge bullets because that would really suck."

"Gimme a gun," I groaned, and then in the next moment my stomach cramped hard, and I was bending over, a violent stream of liquid ejecting out of my mouth across the shitty motel room. It was sudden and brutal, and for me, it seemed to last forever.

Even Louise seemed surprised by the eruption, and after somehow having managed to avoid getting caught in the projectile spray, now edged towards the exit door, holding her breath.

"Is it supposed to hurt this much?" I gasped.

"You'll be fine, really," Louise said, trying not to breathe.

"You're lying aren't you?"

"A little, yeah."

"Scale of one to I hate you-die-die die?"

"So, I'm going to go and try to kill these evil fucks rather than breathe anymore of this because this right here is pure evil."

I threw a half-hearted middle finger salute.

"Love you too, Bob," Louise said and then she slipped out into the corridor, the door clicking shut behind her.

I wanted to look out the window to see where the Gentlemen were, but instead I found myself staggering towards what could only be the bathroom, feeling the sabotaged bio-chemical factory that had replaced my stomach on the verge of a violent eruption. I ripped the sheet-toga away and made it to the toilet a full second before my ass exploded.

Gunfire broke out, a distant rat-tat-tat-tat, followed by a couple of distinctive *blam-blam-blams* of Louise's handgun, but I wasn't listening. I was screaming as my insides tore themselves to pieces in a symphony of pain and misery.

Worst. Dream sequence. *Ever.*

Pro-Tip for Humans #98:
Be more human.

Chapter 13
<u>SO I MIGHT BE A VAMPIRE</u>

I was alive, and goddamn it felt good.

I opened my eyes and realized that for the first time in what felt like forever, I wasn't wishing for death. Let's be absolutely clear on this: I didn't jerk awake and gasp all dramatically and shit, so get that out of your head right now.

Stop it.

I had somehow ended up in the undersized bathtub, shower turned on, water spraying down on my sprawled out and unconscious body, and I realized three things at once: I was alive; I was wet; and I was *cold*.

Oh, wait, I was wrong: *four things*. There was someone banging on the front door.

I clambered to my feet, my legs not trembling like I had expected them to, and looked down at my body, surprised to find it intact, no scars on my side from a stolen kidney or anything fun like a weird and utterly shameful tattoo. That's about how it goes when you have a story about waking up in a strange motel. There *had* been a crazy dream about Louise and some scary vampire dudes, but surely that had been fever-induced.

Bang-bang-bang-bang-bang!

Right: the door.

I pushed aside the Dollar Store shower curtain and instantly regretted it. My nose, traitor that it was, should have warned me about the reality that was waiting for me on the other side of the curtain, but it might have been a firm believer in the 'seeing is believing' principle. I had possibly been sitting in the bathtub for a long time, so my nose and sense of smell had fucked off, and now I had this shit to deal with. Literally.

The floor, walls and toilet were smeared and sprayed with a disgusting and utterly foul mixture of blood, shit and vomit. Seeing the mess seemed to serve as a reminder to my olfactory senses that they had work to do and all at once there was this wall of stink that collapsed over me, triggering my gag reflex. I shoved my finger against my nose, trying to breathe through my mouth, but I could taste it, oh gods I *could taste it*—

I dry heaved, but that was about it. There was nothing in my stomach to eject and only saliva dripped out of my mouth, no matter how hard my stomach muscles clenched.

I almost stepped out of the shower in an attempt to escape the stench but then realized that I would have been stepping directly onto the mess on the floor. Where had all of that filth had even come from? There was no way that *one* person could have had that much shit and vomit *inside* them. There were no clean spots on the floor, and there was absolutely no fucking way I was stepping into that.

Bang-bang-bang-bang-bang!

"Open up! I know you're in there!" a woman's voice yelled, muffled through the doors.

Out of sheer desperation and due to the lack of clean towels, I ripped the shower curtain off the rails and threw it out onto the floor, ignoring the black spots of obvious mildew at the lower edges.

There was something written on the mirror in a shade of bright pink lipstick that seemed oddly familiar. The handwriting was uneven, verging on artistic, and had a heart drawn at the end of it as some type of weird flourish.

THREE DAYS

I would have paused to think about the enormity of that simple statement, that I had been locked in this shitpit of a bathroom for three days, but my need to escape took priority.

Still breathing through my mouth, I carefully stepped out onto the curtain, feeling as my foot pushed the plastic down onto something squishy. Then, trying not to think about it, I took another cautious step, water dripping onto the hideous yellow flowers. One more step and I could reach the door enough to open it, but I did have to balance somewhat precariously as it swung inward. With one mighty push, I lunged out into the relative safety of the room, stumbling and somehow managing not to faceplant into the floor.

Bang-bang-bang-bang-bang!

"I hear you in there! Open up right now, or I'm calling the police!" the woman yelled again.

"Just a minute!" I yelled, or tried to, but my throat was dry and a hoarse croak came out instead. I hadn't used my voice in three days and that takes a toll on anybody. I cleared my throat and tried again. "Be right there!" I managed this time.

I looked around desperately for clothes. There was no way Louise had brought me to this skanky-ass motel completely naked, so my clothes had to be here *somewhere*. I pulled open the closet door and was relieved to see a set of clothes neatly folded on the shelf. Oddly enough, there was a black suit with a white shirt hanging in the closet, the type of clothes I definitely did not wear, so I ignored them and pulled out my jeans from the closet.

Bang-bang-bang-bang-bang!

"Open up now!" the woman yelled again.

"I gotta put some pants on!" I yelled at the door. *"I'm NAKED!"*

I had a moment where I just looked at the huge brownish-red stain on the back of my jeans from where the blood had sheeted down my back, and the absurdity of what had happened and was still happening, hit me full force. I pulled on the pants in a daze, feeling the surreal nature of existence, the hidden syncopation in the bang-bang-banging on the door, and did I need a shirt? No fuck the shirt and goddamit lady stop banging on the goddamn door!

I flipped the security bolt and yanked the door open.

The short Filipino woman on the other side of the door

paused mid-knock, her eyes wide in surprise. She was an older lady with a youthful face, the streaks of silver in her hair the only indicator of her age. That, and the leopard print tights that nobody young would ever go near. She quickly made note of my naked chest and apparently rock-hard abs, and a lecherous smile played on her lips.

What? You try going three days without fluids and tell me you won't look more toned, especially when you're answering the door half-naked. Yes, I may have sucked in my gut a little and tried to look like an underwear model, but what guy doesn't do that?

"Somebody is using all of the hot water in the building!" Silver Streak accused, her accent sharp. "You like to take the long hot showers for three days!"

"I'm all done now, promise," I assured her. Saliva suddenly flooded my mouth, and I realized that I was ravenous. I tried on a smile that didn't feel right and wondered if I could just end this conversation so I could find something to eat.

Silver Streak held up three fingers. "You have room for three more days or you pay more. Cash only!"

"Three days, got it," I agreed.

Silver Streak smiled warmly and pointed two fingers at her eyes while she nodded to me. "I like your eyes. Very nice. Sexy man."

"Thanks?" I said and slowly closed the door on Silver Streak's sudden turn of overtly coming on to me.

What the fuck was that?

And then there it was, the answer looking back at me from the mirror on the wall by the door. I was right about the dehydration causing me to look more buff than I had ever looked, but that wasn't the thing that had caught Silver Streak's attention. No, that had been the pair of brilliant pale-blue eyes that now occupied my eye sockets.

The eyes looking back at me were not the eyes I had grown up with and looked at in the mirror every single day. Oh no, those beloved eyes had been a dark brown, deep and thoughtful, *soulful* as my mom used to say. They had never ever looked like this, these freak eyes that now sat in my eye sockets like they belonged there.

The eyes that stared back at me, no matter how much I rubbed at them with my knuckles, trying to unsee, those eyes were a pale blue, almost luminescent in the dim light of the room.

That was, of course, the point where I freaked the fuck out.

Forget logic, forget pain. Forget sanity, just forget rational thought. Forget who you were or who you might have been. Forget everything, but remember these words because they may be the last words you hear. Forget it all because none of it matters. Forget the story, forget the songs, they were all wrong anyway, all lies planted like a seed of ugliness and fear, to feed the hunger, to feed the growing seed of myth that lies buried deep within. Forget everything you've known because it is *a lie.* Forget the truth and know that you are the truth. *And know that you are also the lie.*

Louise had put my phone into the bedside table drawer. I called Claude.

He picked up on the first ring.

"I'm stone fucking sober, and I might be a vampire," I blurted. Those freaky blue eyes in the mirror threatened to break my mind.

Claude paused for a moment. "There is so much wrong with that sentence. Let's just deal with the vampire part."

"It was Louise. She's a fucking *vampire* man. Something happened, and now I'm supposed to be a vampire, and I don't know where Louise is, and I'm kinda sorta maybe definitely freaking out right now."

"So this isn't you turning into a vampire? You're an actual factual vampire?"

"That's what Louise said—"

"Louise is a *vampire.*"

"Hey! Focus on me right now. I'm the one freaking out here."

"Fine, fine, it's just a bit of a shock, okay?"

"Anyway, after the most fucked up three days in a bathroom that I don't ever want to think about ever again, my eyes are fucking blue! Blue!"

The phone chirped, and I looked at it, wondering what the hell was going on. Claude was calling on Facetime while he was on the phone with me. I tapped the ACCEPT button and his face popped up on the screen. Behind him was what looked like a bank vault or something.

"Holy shit, dude!" Claude exclaimed. "Have you *seen* your *eyes*?"

"Why do you think I'm freaking out?"

"They're just like Louise's eyes…"

"I hope that's you still focusing on me."

"One hundred percent. Wait, that's a lie: ninety-eight percent."

I glared at Claude, and he shrugged unapologetically.

"So where is Louise?" he asked.

"I don't know, man. There was this whole fucked-up dream that maybe wasn't a dream, and I don't know."

Now it was my turn to lie. *The Gentlemen* floated across my thoughts, looking for a terror to connect to, and I felt my heart fluttering in my chest as a wave of lightheadedness struck me along with the urge to run, get the fuck out of there-- I tried very hard to think of anything else. Anything but that. Anything but *them. Just the possibility that they had taken Louise—*

"Isn't this the part where you're supposed to try to convince me that vampires aren't real so we can have a huge fight?" I asked Claude as a means to distract myself.

"I think we're way past that point. Stay put. I'm coming to get you so we can figure out what the fuck is going on"

I almost lost it. I looked around the shitty room, noticing the smear of dried blood and vomit from where I had puked three days ago, and felt a wave of unreality crash over me.

My stomach growled at me, loud and hard, determined not to be ignored. I rifled through the bedside drawer again, already knowing it was empty, but I was still hoping there would be something overlooked and forgotten that I could chew on and fool my stomach into not digesting me from the inside. Nothing.

"I don't even know where I am—"

"You're at a shit hotel on King Street West. The Ni Hao Palace."

I decided that the suit was a better option and rummaged through the pockets. I instantly hit paydirt: a ten dollar bill and a stick of Peppermint gum that was instantly peeled and popped into my mouth.

"How the fuck—" I asked as the most delicious sugar assaulted my senses, intense and sharp and so fucking sweet I was practically rolling my eyes in ecstasy. *Holy shit.*

"Find My Friends app dude. You've been missing for three days. I pinged your phone to alert me as soon as you turned it on."

"How soon can you be here? I feel like I'm losing my mind." But at least the juices from the gum were doing the job of calming my stomach for the moment.

"Ten minutes. Maybe fifteen. You gonna be okay til then?"

"I can chill. I can hold it together. I'm just *really fucking hungry.*"

"Okay, cool. Just try not to bite anyone, okay?"

"Why would I bite anyone?"

"Vampires and biting kinda go hand in hand. Resist the urge!"

"You got it."

"Oh and you might want to call your mom. She's freaking out."

Click, and Claude was gone.

I grabbed my shirt from the shelf, but I could tell that it was a ruined mess even before I touched it. The memory of Brandi biting me on the shoulder came flooding back and and reflexively turned to peer at the wound— the wound that wasn't there. My shoulder wasn't even sore. I rushed to the mirror and examined my neck, and sure enough, it was like it had never happened.

My stomach growled at me again, and I made up my mind. I grabbed the white shirt from the hanger and put it on, marvelling at how nice the shirt felt on my skin as I buttoned it up. It was my size, as if it had been made for me. The jacket was next, and once again it was a perfect fit. There was a moment where I felt utterly stupid as I realized that I hadn't put on the socks and the shoes first, but then I said fuck it, and shoved my feet into the brand new brown leather shoes that had been left for me. Where my Doc Martens had vanished to, I had no idea, but the way the leather of these new shoes felt on my feet made me forget all about those old boots.

I made my way out of the room and down the short corridor, the blare of television sets and people having loud sex behind the paper thin walls a fitting accompaniment and reminder of how shitty this motel was. Thankfully the staircase was open and not closed in, so I didn't have to deal with the stink of urine in the corners as I made my way down to the first floor.

At the bottom of the stairs, I found what I was looking for. Silver Streak was in the process of beating on a battered Candy Machine at the far end of a corridor, illuminated only by the flickering light of a failing fluorescent light. It was one of those machines that was designed to overcharge you for its own existence, a prize for the most desperate.

Silver Streak straightened as I approached, her face lighting up as she realized that it was me. She peeled her Snickers and placed it suggestively against her lips, her tongue flicking out seductively to lick at the chocolate.

My stomach growled and did that clenching thing again where it felt like a fist was squeezing from the inside as the hunger rose. I was mesmerized as I closed the distance, only one thing on my mind, the need to feed. I found myself running my tongue over my top teeth in anticipation, and had my incisors always been that long?

I reached Silver Streak and she looked up at me expectantly, her breath coming shallow now as she looked into my eyes. I had the thought that she must taste like chocolate—

"See something you like?' she asked, and I nodded.

I leaned close to her and she tilted her chin up invitingly, the chocolate bar moving away from her mouth and her glistening red lips.

Leaning closer now, I reached down with one hand, and in one deft movement, plucked the Snickers bar from her hand. Then I opened my mouth wide and bit down onto the chocolate bar, devouring that fucking thing in three bites, chewing noisily, not caring how Silver Streak was looking at me. It was easily the best goddamn chocolate bar I had ever tasted, the chocolate rich and creamy, the nuts delicious and so perfect—

"I can get you more chocolate," Silver Streak breathed at me.

Her face lit up as an idea occurred to her. "It's in my room."

You know what? I almost went with her. There was a moment where she took me by the hand and started to lead me back down the corridor while I was practically high on the explosive flavour of the chocolate. It was orgasmic, and the promise of more chocolate was too much to ignore.

Did you know that chocolate releases the same endorphins as cocaine or heroin? It's in smaller doses with chocolate, but that's what you're really getting high on. The same endorphin release can be triggered by some of those addictive games you find on your phone and app developers have figured it out, so when you say a game is addictive, you aren't kidding.

Anyway, my point here is that I was *literally high on chocolate*. At that moment I would have agreed to anything—

Just like that, my chocolate high faded, and I realized that this Filipino lady had every intention of fucking the shit out of me even if she had to feed me an entire box of chocolate.

"Hey, you own this place, right?"

"Yes, me and my husband, but it's okay, he's not here. Just you and me all over you."

I peeled her wandering hands off me.

"Was there a girl here a couple of days ago? She had eyes just like mine."

That seemed to do the trick. Silver Streak suddenly looked very uncomfortable, eyes suddenly darting around, paranoid.

"I remember her. Very unlucky."

"Why do you say that?"

"They came for her," Silver Streak said with a shudder. "The boogeymen." She frowned at me and sighed deeply then shuffled me towards the door. "You should go now. You look like more bad luck."

In less than a minute I had gone from being lusted after, to being practically shoved out of the dirty glass door at the entrance to the motel. One step back and the motion activated flood lights clicked on, turning the alley into intat daylight and effectively blinging the shit out of me. I cried out and staggered away, hands covering my eyes, unable to see anything but white. Apparently my new eyes had a huge flaw.

The lights clicked off and I blinked rapidly, trying to get my eyes to adjust. I realized after a moment that I was facing the mouth of the alley where those dark men had appeared, half-expecting to find them waiting for me, somehow having tracked me down—

There was a tall dark figure in the alley, his knee length coat adding a familiar menace to the shape of the man, more of a blur than a man due to my malfunctioning eyes.

A spike of fear, no not fear: *terror*, made its way into my heart, and I almost gave into the urge to run for my life, tear my way back into the shitty motel so I could at least have a fighting chance. I heard an audible *snickt* and felt my incisors grow longer, my mouth coming open at the same time to bare my fangs. It was instinctive and scared the shit out of me—

"Holy shit, dude! You have fangs?" Claude exclaimed as he stepped into the light and stopped being that scary motherfucker in the dark.

My hands flew to my mouth, and I felt my incisors retract smoothly as if out of embarrassment. I crossed my eyes trying to see my own damn mouth, then shook it off as reality asserted itself.

"Well, I think that's enough proof," I quipped feebly to Claude. "I'm a fucking vampire."

Pro-tip for Vampires #1:
Read the goddamn manual. You'll thank me later.

Chapter 13
EVERYTHING YOU KNOW
IS A GODDAMNED LIE

The little girl with the unruly hair was driving me crazy. She was all the way across the diner at a booth with her family, and had made several failed attempts to climb over the back of the booth, while her besieged father absent-mindedly reached to haul her down. The fact that he was attempting to talk to the waitress while the girl's little brother repeatedly stabbed the menu and yelled "and fries" at every chance, was a testament to the man's patience. It served only to irritate the shit out of me at the pure *normal-ness* of the scene. Not the other kind of irritating because the kid was irritating, but that it was so fucking *normal*, the kind of normal that I was no longer part of, because hello? *Vampire?*

"Don't you know it's rude to stare?" Claude asked, as he placed the final jam packet in his customary wall of jam.

"I'm not staring," I rebutted, "I'm using my mental powers to make that little girl's head *explode*."

Claude threw a packet of jam at me, and I glared at him instead.

"So, I guess we can rule out mental powers?" he asked, finger hovering over the screen of his phone. He had created an actual spreadsheet of vampire powers organized by psychic, physical, and sexual. When had he even had time to do all of *that?*

"You don't know that," I grumbled and turned to glower at Claude, fingers to my temples.

There was an awkward silence where absolutely anything failed to happen.

"What are you doing now?"

"Trying to set you on fire. With my *brain*!" I intoned in what I thought was a pretty good mystic-sounding voice, worthy of the seediest of fortune-tellers with neon signs in their windows and their own YouTube channels.

"So, no compulsion, no pyrokinesis, no telekinesis--"

My hand flicked out and destroyed the wall of jam bricks. I used my hands to mimic an explosion, complete with sound effects.

"Fwoosh! Ka-boom!"

"Big no to telekinesis," Claude said drily. "I swear, you've got to be the worst vampire I've ever met."

"I'm the *only* vampire you've ever met."

"You and Louise."

"Point taken."

Our waiter swooped in to deposit two cups and a pot of coffee onto the table and was gone before I could properly register his presence. I poured a cup while Claude fiddled around with something on the seat next to him.

The little girl bouncing on the thick red leather seats of the booth caught my attention, and I turned my full glare back on her. My mom would have murdered me if I had even thought about acting that way in a restaurant when I was a kid, and this little girl had the nerve to be *this* awake so late in the evening.

I turned back to Claude. "I should really call Mom--"

Claude chose that moment to shove a submarine-sandwich-sized ornate gold crucifix into my face. From up close, the cross looked like it had cost a fortune, and it was pretty nice as crosses go. The crucified Jesus was a masterclass of detail, the pain and anguish on his face designed to make the viewer as guilty as possible, *because, hey: this is what you did to me you motherfuckers!* It looked well-used, the tarnish only showing in certain areas, the rest of the surface polished probably from continual rubbing and handling.

"Did you steal that from a church?" I asked Claude as I dropped the spoon onto the table. I tentatively poked at the crucifix as if it might bite.

Claude didn't even bother to look guilty. "I was in a rush, okay? I had to improvise. Now stop admiring the damn thing and ignite, or turn to dust, or at least flinch. Come on. Flinch? For me?" Claude flourished the crucifix again. "Aha!"

"Seriously, dude?"

"Ya think? *Now begone foul demon!*"

I slapped the crucifix aside, not sure if I should be hurt or annoyed. Settling for annoyed, I picked up my coffee.

"That was a dick move, dude," I chided him. "Not cool."

"Sorry, I got caught up in the moment." This time Claude flushed red with embarrassment and set the cross down on the table next to the black leather briefcase he had brought in with him. Come to think of it, he had pulled the cross out of the same case as well—

I frowned at him. "Dude—"

Claude produced a simple silver Star of David from the briefcase and confirmed my worst suspicions, it was filled with pilfered religious paraphernalia. I glared at him, unimpressed, and grabbed a packet of sugar.

"I'm suddenly having the urge to bite someone," I glowered and hesitated. *Wait, had I already added sugar?*

Claude deflated. "So nothing then?"

"Not even a tingle."

I was torn between adding the sugar or just risking drinking the coffee without sugar. Choices, choices. *Goddammit, Claude.* I tore open three packets and poured them into the coffee.

"I just want you to know how much you're ruining this for me," Claude grumbled as he rummaged through the case with both hands. "I don't think any of these are going to work either." He emptied a number of velvet bags onto the table, different religious totems and carvings tumbling out with a clatter.

"Did you rob a museum or something?" I asked, amazed at the sheer number.

"Something like that. Don't ask, and just roll with it, okay? There's been a lot of strange jobs recently, and this haul was from one of them. The client is coming for them tomorrow."

I picked up a couple of the totems and examined them. There was a little carving of the Hindu elephant-headed god, whatever his name was, and that one was heavy despite the small size.

"Wow, man, some of these look really old. At least I *think* they look old, but what the hell do I know?"

"Only the best for you, pal," Claude said. "Pity none of them seems to work on you. If Louise were here, we wouldn't have to be doing this."

"She should have left an instruction manual," I sighed. "That would have been useful. I don't even know how to make my damn fangs come back out. I've been trying, and I got *nada*. Nothing. *Ne* fucking *rien*. All I got out of the big vampire transformation were fucking scary eyes and a dumb suit."

"Dumb *Armani* suit," Claude rolled his eyes at me, and I looked down in disbelief. The fabric *was* pretty damn nice on closer examination.

"Well, damn. At least Louise had good taste." I felt remarkably stupid for not putting on the pants and choosing my jeans instead. The last suit I had owned had been off the rack from the Men's Wearhouse and had cost me the grand total of $150 on sale. This Armani suit jacket was a perfect fit, and my sleeves popped exactly like James Bond's.

"No luck reaching her phone?" I asked.

Claude shook his head. "Not yet. She'll show up soon though, and then we can all have a nice long chat about vampires and lying to people, and how she is a vampire and didn't tell us... you know: normal shit like that."

Something had been bothering me, and I spoke slowly, trying to find the right words.

"Maybe she *isn't* a vampire?"

Claude gave me his best *"what the fuck are you saying, and why are you talking to me?"* expression. It's hard to explain what it looks like, but trust me: when you see it, you recognize it.

"Yeah, yeah, I know," I rushed on before he could say anything to break my emerging thoughts. "Just hear me out. None of the religious symbols work on me, so maybe I'm not *actually* a vampire? Maybe I'm something else?"

"Dude. Fangs?" Claude pointed at his teeth.

"Dude. Mirrors." I pointed at our reflection in the glass window next to us where we were both visible. "I can see my reflection."

"Don't be a dumbass. You can't break the basic laws of physics. That mirror thing was always bullshit anyway. Probably made up *by* a vampire. I know if I was a vampire, I'd definitely not want people knowing how to pick me out of a supernatural line-up."

"Or defeat me," I muttered. I mulled that for a moment. "You might be onto something there. The best way to hide the truth is to cover it in bullshit. And even if somebody managed to get it exactly right, who the hell would even know? It would just be so much pop-culture that it eventually becomes myth."

"If you're any kind of traditional vampire, you would've been outta here like your ass was on fire, not just sitting there drinking your coffee."

"I'm not actually drinking it yet. Some idiot keeps interrupting me by shoving religious symbols in my face."

Claude wryly held up a Yin and Yang, and I scowled.

"Oh look," I said dryly, "the idiot's back."

Ba-dum-dum! Claude drummed a short rhythm on the table with his fingers to underscore the point with a flourish. "Everything the movies and books told us about vampires is a lie," he said triumphantly.

"What about the stake in the heart?" I challenged him, but I was distracted by Jimmy the waiter making his way over to our table with our food.

"Dude, that shit works on everybody. Most of the ways to kill vampires would work just as well on humans." Claude pulled out his phone and swiped to bring up a screen. "Over a hundred sites on vampires and none of them agree on the lore."

"A vampire should write a blog. Call it: 'How to Vampire' or some shit like that."

Jimmy laid out the food and departed but I was already digging in to feed my protesting stomach. Flavour exploded in my mouth like a series of orgasmic fireworks, and I just kept shoveling in the food.

Goddamn! Had bacon always tasted this good? I mean I know it's always been good, but this was some next-level bacon Jimmy had brought out to us. Definitely worth an extra tip.

Claude watched me and shook his head. I didn't care what he thought because: *bacon!*

It was when Claude poured Tabasco sauce over his eggs that I stopped shoving food into my face-hole, my nose already itching from the moment he had opened the bottle. For a few seconds, a sneeze threatened. The urge to vomit came back rather strongly, and I found myself shutting down my nostrils in defence and just breathing through my mouth. *Damn, why hadn't I ever noticed just how toxic the smell of the Tabasco was?*

"Your Tabasco sauce is seriously fucking with me, dude."

My voice came out all cracked and hoarse, and I coughed, surprising both Claude and myself. My breath caught in my throat and my chest constricted, as if an invisible gorilla had decided to love me and squeeze me and call me George.

Fucking Tabasco.

Claude looked from me down to his eggs swimming in the Tabasco, and in one movement, he threw a napkin over his eggs, grabbed the plate, and walked it over to the counter, but more importantly, *away* from me. The gorilla eased up a little, allowing me to get enough air to fumble a glass of water to my mouth.

Claude returned, concern written across his face.

"So the Tabasco has more effect on you than any of the religious symbols," he said.

I drained my water and slammed the glass onto the table.

"Let's not do that again, shall we?" I said, and Claude nodded, but I could tell he was filing that information away for later.

I grabbed my coffee and took a huge gulp, not caring that it was still hot, just wanting something to wash away the *feel* of the Tabasco. My throat was raw, as if someone was in the act of scraping my throat with a belt sander.

Flavour overwhelmed my taste buds, but it wasn't like the orgasmic fireworks from the bacon, this was more like a blast of lightning, napalm lit on fire and coursing through my veins with a wicked glee--

Everything went white, as deep in my brain synapses fired and then fired again and *again* and *again* and *again*—

It was all a fog to me, and somewhere I could hear a faint scream, but I was too high to care.

Pro-Tip for Humans #86:
Advice freely given from someone who hates you is
probably going to hurt you.

Chapter 15
DOCTOR, DOCTOR

Reality returned, much like a brick to the face. One minute I was in a happy place with clouds, then boom, I woke in the front passenger seat of Claude's car, dimly aware from the way the passing streetlights zipped past, that we were in the middle of committing several dozen traffic violations.

A spasm jerked my body, and I turned my head to look at my friend, my eyes unable to focus. They had picked up nasty habit of wandering in opposite directions, and it gave me a headache to force them to behave. I blinked a couple of times, which seemed to do the trick. Except now, one eyelid stopped working entirely.

"Wha's happ'ing?" I managed to slur. Apparently my mouth was also taking a vacation. Upon further inspection, it seemed that the rest of my body was as equally unresponsive. I was a ragdoll, held upright only the grace of a seatbelt.

"I'm taking you to the hospital, man." Claude said without taking his eyes off the road. He glided the car around a difficult corner and then continued. "You just had a fucking seizure back there. You might have had a stroke or something." He glanced at me for a moment. "Your eyes and ears were bleeding, dude."

Something popped in my ear, and my eyes finally decided that they wanted to focus on Claude after all. There was a tingly feeling all over my body as nerve receptors started to fire again. I somehow managed to flop one hand up in an attempt to massage my neck.

"I feel like shit. Like I overdosed or something."

"Just stay still, man. I got your back."

"Feeling better already. Really." I slurred.

"She sells silly salty sluts by the seashore. Say it!"

"Brain no like," I sputtered.

By the time we screeched into the hospital entry road, I was fully recovered, but a certain stubborn someone-who-shall-remain-unnamed (Claude), wasn't listening to me. That same someone managed to commandeer a wheelchair, and dumped me into it with more force than necessary. Then humming the theme song to the *Facts of Life* under his breath, he wheeled me into the emergency room, where I expected to spend the next three hours of my life waiting for boredom to slowly kill me.

As soon as we entered, the guard on duty who had a bit of a John Goodman (Big Lebowski era) thing going on, took one look at me and pointed Claude toward a desk where a bored looking black lady sat. There were about a dozen people scattered throughout the waiting room, and more would be coming. According to Louise, Friday nights were always the busiest nights, with all of the whack-jobs simultaneously deciding to engage in risky behaviour. The lady at the desk looked particularly formidable, so I got ready to explain why I didn't have my health card and why I had the number committed to memory. It was a charming story guaranteed to make the nurse not hate me too much.

Claude wheeled me over to the desk, and without looking, the nurse handed a clipboard to him. Claude didn't even pause, just took a pen and started writing, filling out my information as if he too had it fully memorized.

"What happen with him?" Nurse Bradshaw (according to her nametag), asked with a sharp Jamaican accent, and then she saw my eyes, and one eyebrow shot up.

Fuck. I had forgotten about my eyes. I didn't have a story, charming or otherwise to explain *that* anomaly—

Nurse Bradshaw exhaled in a way that clearly said "*not this shit again*" and got up from her chair, picking up what looked more like a price scanner than a medical instrument. There was a *de Biers Instruments* logo on the side, which at first glance it had looked like a little bat, but that must've been an illusion of design.

"Well there's actually a really funny story—" I tried to come up with a good response, but I was already failing.

"Look here, right at me," Nurse Bradshaw said in a no-nonsense tone and raised a finger in front of her nose. I obeyed and found myself looking into the blue light of the scanner. There was a *beep,* and Nurse Bradshaw said, "Uh, huh, thought so."

I glanced back at Claude to see if he found this as odd as I did, but he was of course acting as if this was an everyday occurrence while he filled out the paperwork.

"Raise yuh hand," Nurse Bradshaw said, and proceeded to clip a blue plastic band around my wrist, while at the same time motioning to a passing orderly. "See if yuh can find Doctor Mendelshonn. This is one of them *special* patients."

Claude passed the iPad back to Nurse Bradshaw, and she glanced at it briefly before nodding to the orderly, who just rolled her eyes and led the way through the swinging doors into the maze of examination rooms beyond.

The first time I had actually had to go beyond those doors as a patient, it had been an eye-opening experience. A lot of people think that the main waiting area at the front is the main obstacle and that once you're through the main doors, it's a simple matter of getting treatment. What most don't expect is that there are more waiting areas for less severe cases before you even get to see a doctor. I'm a veteran of emergency rooms all around the city, so I was completely prepared to wait for another three hours despite our speedy progress through triage.

"In case you didn't recognize it, yes, this is the same emergency room that Louise works at," Claude murmured, and I looked around more attentively even though I knew there was almost no chance of Louise actually being there.

The orderly escorted us to an examination room and hooked a thumb towards one of the three empty exam bays, then left without a word. Claude went off to check out the curtained-off bays to make sure nobody was in the room with us.

I couldn't hold it in anymore.

"Did she know I was a vampire?" I hissed at Claude.

"I dunno, man," he admitted. "She knew you were *something*, that's for sure."

"I've never actually gotten through the front so fast before," I blurted out. " The eye scan thing was kind of new—"

"You've been in the ER way too many times if you know the procedure so well."

"Not really that many," I said evasively. "I hang out with some *stupid* people when *you're* off doing your heists. You have no idea how many times stoned people think it's a great idea to do home renovations while tripping balls."

Claude frowned thoughtfully. "The thing that gets me is that they seem awfully well-prepared for someone like you. Like there are a lot more vampires around than you'd think—"

The door at the far end opened and a short blonde woman bustled in, lips pursed, brilliant pale-blue vampire eyes curiously appraising us. Her name tag read Dr. Iva Mendelsohnn, something that I realized I could read from twelve feet away.

Apparently I wasn't going to need to wear glasses for a very long time. *Upgrade!*

Dr. Mendelshonn noticed Claude, and a smile broke across her face as she decided she liked what she saw. She liked it *a lot* as a matter of fact.

"What seems to be the problem?" she asked and then cocked her head, confused at what she was seeing. "Are you wearing coloured contacts?"

"I'm not the patient," Claude pointed out and stepped aside so she could see me better.

"Hi. I had a bad reaction from some coffee?" I waved helpfully.

Dr. Mendelshonn looked from Claude down to me where I was trying my best to look like the obvious patient. Her smile faded as she saw my eyes, and she sighed the deepest of sighs. She gestured to the bed indicating that I should sit, and I complied readily, trying hard not to fanboy all over her. *Wow! An actual vampire!*

Dr. Mendelsohnn was all business as she examined me. "I'll be honest," she said, "I haven't seen an *Accidental* in a long time. Harry's pretty much put a stop to that, and we *especially* don't see your type."

"And what type is *that* exactly? *Black*?" I said evenly, my eyes narrowed to a slit as I prepared for whatever toxic bullshit she was about to spew.

To her credit, Dr. Mendelshonn blinked in surprise and sudden self-awareness. She shook her head in solemn horror. "Oh no, sweetie: I just meant that you were too poor to be a vampire."

Surprise threw a bucket of cold water on my anger, which was undergoing an identity crisis as it struggled with the decision to turn into indignation or shame turning into indignation. All I could say was: "Oh."

Even Claude was stunned. "Are you sure you're even a doctor?"

She pointed at Claude. "This one was *made* to be a vampire. He looks like he was *born* in that suit. He's the type that goes through the program with a silver spoon in his mouth and comes out looking like what people want their vampires to look like: Tall, dark and yummy." She turned her attention to me. "You, well, you're common as muck, as ordinary as they get. You weren't recruited: you were rescued. Ergo: Accidental."

"How can you be so sure he's an Accidental?" Claude said defensively, and Dr. Mendelsohnn smiled ruefully.

"You guys are here because he had an embolism from drinking coffee," she pointed out. "It's kind of a day one lesson. Now, anybody got more stupid questions?"

"You just made me lose all excitement about meeting other vampires," I admitted. "I was about to fanboy all over you."

"You're so fresh out the grave it's sweet."

"The grave?" I said incredulously, my brain reeling. "Are actual *graves* involved?" Another stunning thought occurred to me. *"Are we the undead?"*

Dr. Mendelsohnn reached out and pinched the skin on my bicep, hard. I yelped at the sudden stinging pain, pulling away from her.

"Just be glad that wasn't a scalpel. You bleed, you feel pain, you have to eat actual food. You shit, you piss, and you sweat. Guess what? You're still alive. Just different now, so no more of this undead shit, okay?

"Just be glad that wasn't a scalpel. You bleed, you feel pain, you have to eat actual food. You shit, you piss and you sweat. Guess what? You're still alive. Just *different* now, so no more of this undead shit, okay?"

"I'm sorry, but everything I know about vampires is from books and movies, okay? I'm just a little bit fucked up over the impossible fact that vampires exist outside of pop-culture and that is one serious mind-fuck."

Dr Mendelsohnn raised a finger in warning, apparently knowing what was coming.

"Do *not* ask me about *werewolves.*"

"But I wasn't about to ask you about werewolves," I mumbled. I was totally lying.

Claude raised his hand. "I'd like to ask about werewolves."

Dr. Mendelsohnn snapped the cover on her iPad shut and wheeled on us, stabbing a well manicured finger at Claude, then at me, pretty much whoever she decided was pissing her off more.

"Let's get one thing clear here. I am not your magic fucking elf. I'm not here to dispense wisdom and tell you all the shit that you don't know about being a vampire. I'm e*specially* not here to send you off on some grand adventure, so fuck you and especially fuck you." That last one was to me. "It's the same with all you Accidentals, I swear it. You want to learn how to be a vampire so bad, then go find whoever turned you and tell them I sent you—" Her eyes narrowed as she made a connection. She looked around the empty room and all of the arrogance and righteous anger went out of her. For the first time, she actually looked vulnerable. *Human.*

"Oh, goddamit," Dr Mendelsohnn said with sudden realization. "It was Louise wasn't it?"

The silence spoke louder than we ever could.

"We were kinda hoping someone here had seen her," I admitted.

"Did you see if they came for her?" Dr. Mendelsohnn asked so quietly that I almost didn't hear her.

"If who came—"

"The *Gentlemen!*" she snapped, eyes blazing, and I nodded under the force of her anger.

Claude glanced at me, a question in his eyes, since I had avoided telling him about the Gentlemen and now this more experienced vampire was terrified of the men I had avoided mentioning. I looked somewhere else, pretending not to see.

"She's okay," I whispered hoarsely. "She has to be."

Dr. Mendelsohnn sighed deeply and bitterly. She barely contained her anger as she spoke.

"Dilute your coffee, three to one ratio, avoid getting your head chopped off, but first: get the fuck out of my hospital."

***

We got the fuck out of her hospital. If music had been allowed over the intercom system instead of silence broken up by different calls and pages for doctors, I was sure the universe would be mocking me with a song from Jaime's Infinite Playlist. Maybe 'Loser' from Beck, or Radiohead's 'Creep', just to make things interesting.

"You look like you have a plan," Claude noted as we walked toward the exit.

"That's because I kinda sorta do," I admitted.

"Is it a good plan?"

"I have no idea, but that's never stopped me before."

"Fair enough," Claude said with a shrug. "So wanna tell me where we're going?"

I would have stopped and taken off my sunglasses at that point just to be dramatic, but I had glanced back over my shoulder and had spotted Dr. Mendelsohnn watching us from down the corridor, so that almost threw me off my stride.

"We're going to have to go back to the scene of the crime," I said. "Where I died."

Pro-tip for Vampires #4:
Advice from vampires will probably kill you.

Chapter 16
ENEMIES MAKE THE BEST FRIENDS

I f you think that showing up on the doorstep of the place where you died three days before is no big deal, I suggest that you try it for yourself sometime. I had already been caught off guard by the sweat that suddenly appeared on my forehead and the boiling sensation in my stomach. The urge to turn and walk away, because this was clearly not a good idea, had almost taken over, but I had persisted and knocked. The sight of Robert's stupid fucking handsome face as he opened the door was what pushed me over the edge, if I can be completely honest with you. Maybe it was the purple fucking cardigan that did it, I dunno.

Whatever it was, I gave into the surge of hatred and righteous fury that swelled up inside, and I punched that motherfucker right in his perfect fucking nose.

"Fuck!" Robert screamed as he staggered back into the house, blood streaming from his broken nose.

I stormed into the house, leaving an extremely confused-looking Claude behind. He had his mouth open as if he had been about to say something when I punched Robert, so he had kinda been left hanging.

"Bet you didn't expect to see me again motherfucker!" I yelled at the retreating Robert who left a trail of blood droplets in his path. I took another swing, but he saw this one coming and staggered out of range.

"You're supposed to be *dead!*" Robert protested as he backed into the living room, putting a couch between us. I flashed on a memory of shadowy figures fucking like crazy in that same room, which was immediately followed by the thought that this was one room where a blacklight should never ever be used. There was a blonde woman in a very stylish white suit, sprawled facedown on the couch in a classic *'I'm fucking drunk so don't fuck with me'* pose. Robert ignored her so I chose to as well.

"Because you *killed* me!" I accused.

Claude stopped at my side and blinked rapidly as he tried to play catch up. "Wait, he did?"

"What the fuck are you *talking* about?" Robert asked, appearing almost as clueless as Claude, but with a side of righteous indignation.

"I only just remembered! You *killed* me, you asshole!"

"Nope, nope, nope! I was trying to save your dumb ass!" Robert yelled back.

I hesitated, doubt and fragmented memories clouding my conviction. "But I remember—"

"You were so fucking high, you fell off the goddamn table and somehow stabbed yourself in the neck with a scalpel," Robert explained, head and shoulder drooping as if he was too tired for this bullshit. "By the time Louise and I got back, you had just about completely bled out. There was nothing I could do for you."

Okay, I know you're asking yourself, almost literally *'what the fuck? Why doesn't Bob remember how he died when he so eloquently described the details of his death earlier.'* Here is where I remind you that this story is told in hindsight. In the few seconds that it took between Robert opening the door and me seeing his face, my imagination had worked overtime to fill in the huge blank in my memory of that night, and had made some stunning leaps of logic that were obviously and fatally wrong, leading to a seriously fucked up situation. This isn't a murder mystery: it's a comedy of errors.

Now, back to your regularly scheduled programming.

Claude had examined the room around us, which looked

quite different with the lights. The large living room was immaculately designed and looked almost exactly like an Ikea display, down to the little knick-knacks that looked like nobody had ever touched them. However there was something off about the room and Claude had figured it out while I was busy pointing the finger at the wrong murderer.

"You're leaving town," Claude stated, and both Robert and I looked at him, Robert a little more cautiously, almost as if he had been caught doing something wrong.

"Who the *fuck* are you again?" Robert finally spat.

"The guy who's asking why you have three hastily-packed suitcases waiting at the bottom of the stairs as if you're in a rush to go somewhere," Claude said evenly, pointing to the incriminating evidence. "You have drawers open all over the place as if you're looking for something and don't have enough time to close them. Ergo, you look like a man who is running for his life, so I gotta wonder why. Or perhaps the better question is, who are you running from?"

Robert focused his light-blue vampire eyes on Claude, a sudden intensity and focus on his face. "*Forget about it. It's nothing.*"

Claude raised an inquisitive eyebrow, meeting Robert's steady focus. He looked almost amused. "Hey, Bob, is he really trying to Jedi mind-trick me?"

"I kinda think he is," I mused. I turned my attention to Robert who was unusually focused. "Is that what you're doing?"

"YES!" Robert snapped, not breaking eye contact with Claude, but my friend didn't explode or catch on fire or start break-dancing. Robert finally looked away, flustered. "Goddamit, I'm losing my touch."

"Sorry, not sorry?" Claude said.

"So vampires can use Jedi mind tricks to make people do shit? Can you teach me the ways of the Force?" I asked Robert, excited by the possibility. "But in a way that actually works?"

Robert threw his hands in the air. "Fuck you man. Fuck both of you."

The blonde woman slid off the couch and sat upright, one blue vampire eye bleary and completely drunk. The left eye was covered with a black leather eye-patch. She looked at us and clambered to her feet.

"Don't mind me," Blondie muttered, and stumbled out of the room. After a moment there came the clatter and clink of someone in the kitchen and Robert shrugged at us.

"It's actually her house," Robert said by way of explanation.

"So who are you running from?" Claude asked.

Robert glared at both of us and then shook his head. "Look man, everything is seriously fucked up right now. Somebody *died* at my party and it's attracting all the wrong kinds of attention. Yes, I'm skipping town, and maybe you should do the same, you know, before you show up on anybody's radar. Check out the scene in New York. They got a decent community, they're a little less uptight about rules, and they have non-extradition laws, so—"

"Where is Louise?" I asked quietly.

A bottle smashed in the next room, and Blondie laughed drunkenly. "Oops!" she muttered.

Robert glanced toward the kitchen and then back at me, suddenly shifty. "Well… Louise is the one who got Beatrice to help turn you, right? That's like one of the biggest no-nos in the Vampire world. Well, that and killing another vampire."

Claude and I exchanged an uneasy look. The hair rose on my arms and a sick feeling coiled in the pit of my gut.

Robert shrugged and glanced at his suitcases, apparently ready to be done with this shit. "Look, you don't go around making vampires. *Ever.* That's one of the big ones. Harry'll sic the Gentlemen on any offender for sure. And if *they* already got to her, no one's seeing her ever again."

"You don't know Louise," Claude blustered. "She's smart, she's resourceful—"

"She's so fucking dead," Robert scoffed. "You forgot that one." He reached up and adjusted his nose with an audible click and a hiss of pain.

Claude lunged at Robert, totally losing his cool for the first time that I had seen in ages. I don't know if I saw his attack coming, but I found myself tackling him and lifting him easily off his feet to keep him away from the sneering Robert. Since when had I gotten that strong?

"You don't have to be an asshole about it!" I snapped at Robert. "She's our friend!" I released Claude.

The asshole backed away to the other side of the room. "I liked Louise too, but facts is facts man."

"This whole attitude right here is because I punched you, isn't it?"

"That and because I don't like you."

"I want to punch him again," I told Claude. "Can I punch him again?"

"Don't look at me," Claude replied. "You didn't ask me the first time."

Robert sneered at the both of us. "You got lucky man. Don't push it." He strode over to his waiting luggage. "We're done here. I'd like to get the fuck out of town if it's all the same to you."

"Are they coming for you?" Claude asked Robert. "The Gentlemen?"

"Maybe," Robert said shiftily as he made his way to the entrance with his luggage. "If your friend here had any sense, he would run before they came looking for him. Either that or off himself. They don't like Accidentals, like *at all.*"

Blondie sauntered back into the hallway and chugged from a bottle of vodka as if it was water. I watched in admiration for a second before something occurred to me.

"Hey, before you go, could you at least give me a few tips on being a vampire? I don't know fuck all about any of this shi,t and you're the only other vampire I know..."

Robert paused at the door. "Shoulda thought of that before you hit me," he replied smugly, then relented. "Look, the most important thing you have to know is that blood isn't food, and that you only need a little, so don't go around killing people like a goddamn psycho. That's one way to end up dead for sure."

Robert considered me and sneered. "I could tell you more... but one: I ain't got ten years; and two: I really don't want to."

"Wait," I said, stunned by this offhand revelation, "we actually *drink* blood? I haven't even felt the urge to bite anybody or anything."

"That's only because you haven't had it yet," Robert called back over his shoulder as he walked away. "You'll see!"

"There's so much I can learn from you!"

"Go fuck yourself!"

The car roared to life a moment later.

"So what now?" Claude asked.

"Who the fuck is Beatrice?"

Blondie belched long and hard and we both turned to look at her.

"Who's asking?" Beatrice said and promptly fell over into a drunken heap.

***

Ten minutes later Beatrice was in the process of raiding the gigantic hoard of liquor in the pantry, while Claude and I hovered outside the kitchen door trying to figure out our best course of action. Correction: Claude tried to figure out our course of action while I watched Beatrice, utterly fascinated.

She had found a bowl of Sweet N' Sour Gummy Worms, and one of them dangled from her lips, its multi-coloured striped body swaying from the movement. All the bottles in Robert's liquor cabinet were gallon-sized and from the way Beatrice gleefully hauled the bottles onto the countertop, it seemed she was determined to drink them all.

"You sure this is a good idea? I'm not comfortable leaving you alone with her."

"I'm all out of ideas and vampires."

"Try not to piss this one off will ya? I'm gonna go call back my new client. He's been blowing my phone up all night."

Claude exited out the front door, already on the phone. I took a deep breath and approached Beatrice cautiously. She

168

had found a gallon bottle of vodka and now chugged steadily, putting several frat houses to shame in a single moment. Her one uncovered eye turned to look at me as I approached, and she held up a finger to indicate I should wait. So I watched with reverence as she polished off the bottle and then followed up that performance with the kind of belch that would have instantly made her the undisputed king of all frat houses, for the sheer intensity and volume. That this kind of behaviour was coming from a stunningly attractive woman who was model-tall—easily over six-feet—and who apparently didn't give a fuck what anybody thought of her, was nothing short of amazing. Girls who looked like that were usually all prissy, at least in my experience.

Beatrice turned her decidedly drunk eye on me and threw me a crooked grin. "Talk fast so I can decide how much I don't not hate you." She paused as she worked through the obvious double negatives, decided she liked it and grinned.

What the hell? I got the feeling absolute honesty was going to be the best course of action. "I need someone to train me before I end up dead."

"Oh, I dunno," Beatrice slurred, her eyes dropping to my crotch. "You'd make a cute corpse."

"Which is exactly the opposite of what I'm going for."

"Ha! And you're funny too!" Beatrice reached out, fast as a snake and grabbed my loins, snagging my dick with amazing accuracy. She looked surprised for a moment and then smiled as I tried and failed not a squirm. "Do you want to fuck me?"

That caught me completely off guard. "We just met!" I squealed like a prissy sorority girl.

"Not an answer!" Beatrice snarled and squeezed the hell out of my junk. I whimpered, and she leaned close to whisper in my ear. "I have something you need. Aren't you supposed to be nice to me?"

She gave an extra squeeze on the word "nice," just for emphasis.

"This is not helping!" I managed to gasp, and Beatrice relented. I cradled my crotch and sank to the floor, the second wave of pain that came from the blood rushing back into the offended parts, flooding through me somehow worse than that from being squeezed.

"Don't go anywhere. I gotta go pee the pee of the god damned."

Beatrice strode away, the surprisingly solid heels of her boots, thumping and then stumbling their way across the polished wood floor. The door creaked open and Beatrice slumped onto the toilet and peed like a horse as I watched. Amazing: twenty seconds after meeting the woman and we were already at stage three of a long term relationship.

"Tell ya what," Beatrice called out, still noisily emptying her bladder. "You show me you got what it takes to survive in this fucked up vampire hellscape, and you got a deal. I'll train you." She finished peeing and flushed. I looked up from my position on the floor as she exited the bathroom, appreciating that my balls were no longer throbbing as much but wondered how long that was going to last. I watched as she made her way over to the counter and opened up a fresh gallon bottle of whiskey.

"Are you going to punch me in the dick this time?"

"Nah, I got something much worse in mind. Sun's coming up in a couple of hours. Survive that. Prove to me what it is that Louise saw in you that was worth saving, and then we'll talk."

"Sunrise? Wait, don't we turn into dust in the sunlight or something?" I asked desperately.

"There's only one way to find out," Beatrice said and offered me the open bottle of whiskey. "Drink?"

"The way this day is going, I'm going to need something stronger," I muttered. "Got any coffee?"

***

Claude was still on the phone as I exited the house. I'd like to imagine that I was doing my most badass walk, the type of walk where your crew has no choice but to fall into step behind you. I felt invigorated and full of purpose, and for the first time in what felt like forever, I wasn't afraid.

My epic walk must have caught Claude's attention, because he turned to me and hung up from his call.

"Good talk?"

"Pretty okay. She didn't even punch me in the nuts so that's a win in my book."

Claude turned and joined my march onward, matching me step for step. We were each other's crew, a crew of two, just me and Claude, and that was okay.

"So what's the plan?" Claude asked.

"We're going to greet the sunrise."

"Seriously?"

"Yeah. Apparently if I manage to do it and survive, I've got myself a vampire Yoda to teach me the ways of the force or whatever."

Claude eyed me like I was crazy or something. "Seriously? Won't you ignite into a towering inferno of vampire bits?"

"Look, I gotta do it. For Louise!"

Claude shook his head and rolled his eyes. "Okay, fine. But we're stopping by my place on the way."

"Sure, but why?"

"We're gonna need a fire extinguisher."

Pro-tip for Vampires 8:
Most things that kill vampires also work on humans.
Most things...

Chapter 17
RUN, RUN, HERE COMES THE SUN

The sun came up in the same way as it always does, which is to say slow as fuck, or glacially if you prefer a more poetic description. Waiting in the courtyard of the apartment building for this truly non-cinematic sunrise was a newly-minted vampire (me) and the guy who apparently should have been the real vampire, my best friend (Claude). Claude held a fire extinguisher, while I posed dramatically with one hand in the direction of the rising sun, half-expecting to turn into dust or burst into flames at any moment. It was a terrible time to be atheist, since I didn't have any kind of god to pray to or even swear at.

As much as I was purposely and aggressively poking fate in the eye, neither of those things happened and continued to fail to happen.

I grinned excitedly at the anxiously waiting Claude and gave him the double thumbs-up.

"I'm okay!" I said, grinning like a maniac. "This is fine! Beatrice was just yanking my chain. Nothing is happening!"

Claude waggled the primed and loaded fire extinguisher that was aimed right at my face just in-case me not being on fire stopped being a thing. "Nothing at all?" Claude asked.

"Well, I can feel a slight tingle, like goosebumps, but I'm good! This vampire thing is going to be easier than I thought!"

If you've never sat up to experience the sunrise, then you have no idea just how long it takes. It's not like in the movies where outside is pitch black and then the sun pops up over the horizon, blasting the land with enough light to incinerate any vampires who were dramatically posing at that critical moment after the hero of the story had uttered some pithy catchphrase. It takes much, much longer than that. It's a gradual thing where the sky slowly brightens, the shadows retreating, revealing more and more, until you can clearly see every detail. If you happen to be in the courtyard of an apartment building like mine, you don't even get to see the actual sun for a while as the sky goes from black, to murky purple before making its way to a deep blue.

A line of sunlight slowly widened and made its way down the buildings across the courtyard. It would eventually take over most of the courtyard, but not until around 10 AM.

I laughed like a maniac and did the standard issue Canadian dance-of-joy before I turned said grin on Claude. "Do you know what this means?"

Claude steadied the fire extinguisher and glanced at the slowly spreading sunlight. "That you're forming a conclusion without complete evidence?"

"Are you kidding?" I laughed. "*Look* at me."

"You're still in the shadows, dude, that's hardly conclusive—"

"Seriously? It's daylight, and I haven't turned into dust. That's not conclusive enough for you? You're the one who insisted on being cautious and not doing this on the roof—"

"You wanted to strip down *naked*—"

"Go bold or go home!"

"Oh my god, after twenty years I finally realise that you are a complete idiot."

"Nothing you can say is going to ruin this moment for me! *Nothing*! ARGH!"

The 'argh!' was the result of the sun choosing that exact

moment to hit a window that happened to be perfectly angled to hit me right in the eyes. There was a flash of light and pain, my vision going white from the intensity, and I staggered blindly, blinking rapidly.

"I'm blind! Fuuuuuuck!"

"Dude, you okay?" Claude asked cautiously.

"Am I on fire?" I asked, as the goosebumps spread. The tingles were everywhere, even the soles of my feet. I risked opening my eyes, and Claude slowly faded into view from a field of white as my eyes adjusted.

"No fire," Claude responded.

I laughed defiantly, and found the sliver of reflected sunlight in the courtyard. I raised my middle finger and stuck it into the sunlight, the tingles in my hand growing into something more like a mild electrocution. Still, there was no immolation, so I counted it as a win.

"Fuck you sun!" I declared triumphantly and grinned at Claude. "Who's the idiot now?"

"Um dude... your hand is on fire."

I cocked my head at crazy Claude. Clearly he was speaking a foreign language.

"Say-who-what-now?"

Turning to look at my burning hand was all it took to make it real. I hadn't even noticed that it had been on fire because the thought was just absurd. Once I turned and saw the blistering and boiling flesh that was cracking and turning black under the dancing flames that had engulfed my hand, denial became impossible.

In my memory, it's always like it's happening to somebody else. I freaked the fuck out, and I ran, forcing Claude to run after me, trying to blast me with fire-retardant. And no, I didn't stop drop and roll, because what the fuck use was that when it's your *head on fire*?

Didn't I mention that my head also caught on fire? Well it did. I don't remember the moment it happened. All I know is that I was burning, and I wanted it to stop. Look, running around like a wild turkey made sense at the time. Don't judge me.

Claude finally blitzed me with the fire extinguisher as I stumbled through the open front door into my apartment, and collapsed on the kitchen floor in a cloud of fire-retardant foam.

Claude yelled something at me, but I wasn't listening, only aware of the intense pain that was my skin, only caring about the agony was that my *entire fucking existence.*

I raised my burned hand, mentally preparing myself to see a charred stump . The right side of my face screamed at me in a sizzling kind of way, and the smell of burnt bacon and greasy smoke assaulted my nose. My hand was no longer a source of searing pain, which either meant that it was useless or that there was something going on—

"Claude!" I managed to groan, my hand held out towards him. "My hand!" My voice was raw, and it hurt my throat and my face to speak, but it had to be done.

"Nine-one-one. What is your emergency?" A woman said from over a phone. Claude turned to me, his eyes wide with concern as he held the phone up to his ear, and then he saw what I was showing him.

"I'll have to call back," Claude said to the phone and hung up, staring at my hand.

"Tell me this is real, dude," I said, my voice a little less croaky. The skin on my face wasn't screaming bloody murder at me anymore, and if what was happening to my hand was real, then I knew exactly why that was.

My hand should have been a charred and useless lump. The skin had been burned black, right down to the muscle, as if the fire had been coming from inside. It wasn't a surface burn either, the kind that you could almost walk away from: it had been the kind of burn that reached down into my soul and said fuck you, you motherfucking motherfucker, this hand is mine now, motherfucker. And yet, there I was holding the hand up, skin blackened and cracked, and I was able to move and bend my fingers. There was a flare of pain, but nothing like what I had just gone through with it on fire. Agony, too much feeling as a matter of fact, nerve endings suddenly alive and screaming all at once, a buzz of static-electricity and sharp searing pain as the flesh regenerated—

I screamed the kind of scream you find in comic books—the ones with lots of exclamation marks and vowels. Before this moment, I'd never experienced a full-on comic book wail of agony, but now unfortunately I knew I continued screaming while watching, as my flesh regenerated and healed, the burnt crispy bits falling away. I was unable to look away and all I could think was that this wasn't at all like in the movies. It wasn't like watching a video in reverse at all, it was something else entirely, and it hurt worse than being burned—

I'm going to say it loud so everyone in the back can hear. Ready?

Fuck the movies.

"Bob, look at me," Claude said. "Don't look at your hand, just look at me. It's better if you don't watch."

"How the hell would you know?" I managed to gasp, but I had to look at him to say it.

"Just take it in a little at a time, and you can do this. Get through the next ten seconds okay?"

"Are you fucking kidding me?"

"You're healing, dude, but you just gotta make it through. If you can do this you can do anything, okay?"

"Ten seconds?"

"Ten seconds."

"Just tell me something. How bad do I look right now?"

"You don't wanna know."

"I'm asking aren't I?"

"Yeah, but I figure if you really wanted to know, you'd be asking me for a mirror instead of for my expert opinion."

I reached up to my face and a huge chunk of burned skin flaked off in my hand. I began to freak out again as my damaged arm remembered that my nerve endings were exposed.

"Keep looking at me!" Claude snapped, and I obeyed, trying to control my breathing. "Ten seconds! Ready?"

I nodded, and then we counted together as I focused on nothing but the numbers, ignoring the searing pain that wanted to overwhelm me, drown me and completely take over. When we got to ten, we started again, and then again. And again.

We might have stayed like that for hours. After a while, time had no meaning. It was just the two of us getting through the next ten seconds together, and eventually, it didn't hurt so much anymore. Somehow, we made it through to the other side.

But first we started with ten seconds.

∗∗∗

I passed out on the couch at some point, my hand healed, pale brown and baby smooth and looking like I had gotten the world's smoothest arm transplant surgery. For some reason, the story about the axe popped into my head. You know the one about the axe that had killed a dude and then had the axe-head replaced, then the handle, until it wasn't even the same axe anymore. Yeah I know, I know, you don't get it either, but that was just where my head was at. Hell, I couldn't even take any pleasure from peeling off any of the dead skin, even though it came off in huge translucent flakes that would normally have been very satisfying to peel.

Claude woke me at one point, and I stayed still long enough for him to shave my head with an electric buzzer. Watching the burnt and crispy clumps of hair fall around me like flurries of negative snow, was an unreal experience, dreamy almost. It felt like it should have been happening to somebody else.

That got me looking at my healed arm again and freaked me out a little with the revelation that it was like parts of me were being replaced with vampire parts. I was losing pieces of my humanity and I really wasn't ready for that.

As I drifted into unconsciousness, listening to Claude moving about the apartment, I idly thought that if I slept all day like the vampires in the movies, maybe it wouldn't be such a bad thing.

Let's get one thing out of the way here: I didn't sleep like the dead or whatever. Daylight did fuck-all for keeping me asleep, no matter that the stories say.

My problem was that I woke to a nightmare.

Pro-tip for Vampires #17.
Other vampires want to kill you.

Chapter 18
<u>MONSTERS IN EXPENSIVE SUITS</u>

Remember that dream I told you about? The one I never ever have about an unknown assailant grabbing me by the legs and dragging me from the bed and across the floor before I could properly wake up? That one? Well I was having it again.

Don't worry, this isn't a dream sequence. It's actually something much, much stupider. Ladies and gentlemen, I present to you a play-by-play repeat of an earlier experience.

When the pillowcase was finally ripped from my head, I was not even slightly surprised to find the familiar faces of Tanya and Doreen sneering down at me. They'd already pulled this same attack once, so the element of surprise was gone. I had only seen them once in the past six months, and I still blame them for Jaime breaking up with me, so this wasn't the best of reunions. Especially since it was exactly like last time. In my opinion, if you're going to go around brutalizing sleeping men, you really ought to apply yourself to the task. Use some imagination.

After Tanya and Doreen were petrified by Claude's connections last time, I had honestly never expected to see them again. Julio had made some half-assed apology about some kind of fucked-up loyalty test, but I had been too fucked-up over Jaime to really give a shit.

And yet, for some reason, they had decided that terrorizing me again was a good idea.

"You know Claude is going to have to kick your asses now, right?" I asked, my nonchalant demeanor completely hiding the huge surge of relief I had felt when I realized my attackers were human.

"Don't bother looking for your friend," Tanya said. "He left ten minutes ago, so we got you all to ourselves."

"Lucky me," I replied.

"Julio sent us to offer you an invitation," Tanya smirked. "It's the kind of offer you're not allowed to say no to. He wants you to stash some product for a week."

"Please don't say no," Doreen said helpfully.

"Can I go with option B and tell you both to go fuck yourselves?" I said. "Julio and I already had this conversation two months ago. We have an agreement where we don't fuck with each other, and you assholes are supposed to pretend that I don't exist."

"Doreen, why don't you be a darling and hit him for me," Tanya said with a smile.

Doreen's fist came at my face, but time seemed to slow to a crawl, and it was as if her fist was slogging through Karo syrup. It was still coming at my face, just very, very slowly. I moved my head out of the path, really more as a means of getting a better view of this perplexing situation—

Doreen yelped as her fist smashed into the floor where my face had been only seconds earlier, and pull it back with a hiss, shaking her hand and wincing. Somewhere in the middle of all of that pain, she caught sight of something completely unexpected and turned to face it, her damaged hand seemingly forgotten for the moment. "Who the fuck are you guys?"

I can say that I half expected to hear Claude's voice, but that's just me lying to myself. Even looking back now, it's hard not to lie to myself. It's a gift.

"We have business with Mister Diego," a man's voice said, and terror sliced through me like cold daggers of doom. It was the kind of voice that you listened to and prayed that you would still be alive when it was done talking. Of course it had a British accent. "Why don't you take your friend into the bathroom and beat her to death for me?"

Doreen turned, and there was a moment where all I saw was this strange smile on her face as she turned and grabbed Tanya by the hair and punched her in the face, one, two, three times, knocking her the fuck out. That done, Doreen dragged her lover by the hair into the bathroom and slammed the door shut.

I was only aware of that in the periphery, more as a side note if you will. At the time, I was scrambling to my feet, knowing only that I needed to escape, to get the fuck out of there, because they weren't coming for me anymore, they were here, the Gentlemen were *here*—

It is like a dream, when they come for you.

Nobody tells you that even though you will try to escape, that is completely futile. You will be consumed by the terror of what's coming. You can only watch—a passenger in your own skull, wishing that this is happening to someone else.

Even in my terror, I remember that there are three of them.

An immaculate and beautiful Italian leather shoe is the **first** *thing I see of the leading vampire, but that is quickly followed by the figure of a tall, slim Chinese man, his face ageless, his pale blue vampire eyes burning in intensity and purpose. His lips are thin and cruel, but that is by design as if he is telegraphing to everyone that he has never laughed a day in his life and will murder them for trying to make him laugh. He wears a long black coat that I have seen once before in the alley a few nights before. His suit is most assuredly made of the finest of fabrics that befits a Gentleman of his stature.*

It is a wonder that he is not drinking a cup of tea just to indicate to anyone watching just how much he is not to be fucked with.

A huge gorilla of a man, easily seven-feet tall with arms the approximate size of tree-trunks, follows immediately behind, carrying a chair from my kitchen in one oversized hand. *There is no way someone that huge should look graceful; it's like watching someone in a fat suit, the ease of movement completely disconnected from his bulk. It isn't fat on this man, just pure massive comic-book style muscle. His blue eyes indicate that he is also a vampire, but holy shit, he is unbelievable, as a man or as a vampire.*

I look for the third one, expecting to see his twitchy and restless form materialize behind the large vampire, but nothing of the sort happens. It is only after a moment that I freeze, realizing that I can feel hot breath on the back of my neck and hear the ragged breathing of the third vampire somehow impossibly and terrifyingly behind me. I know in that instant that the only right move to make is none at all, or I will find my guts spilled across the floor before I can react.

Do not turn. Do not pass GO.

I find myself praying fervently that this isn't the moment Claude chooses to return, because I'm sure they'd kill him too, just for fun

The tall Chinese man sits at the same instant that the Gorilla places the chair behind him. It is so smooth it is almost as if they were mentally in sync, the chair clopping down, the Gorilla stepping back, the button on the Chinese Gentleman's jacket coming undone as he adjusts himself. All perfectly timed to a private rhythm.

"My name is Mister Flynn," *the Chinese man introduces himself.* "I, along with my associates Mister Bryce," *he indicates the huge Gorilla behind him,* "and Mister Sinnel," *a nod to the unseen lurking monster behind me,* "are currently seeking the whereabouts of your friend, Louise. You will tell us where she is."

I realize then that I can hear the sounds of Doreen choking Tanya to death in the bathroom. Tanya is not giving up without a fight, but she is still losing. Neither of them have a choice in their fate, and it occurs to me that I also have no choice. The witty comeback that comes to my lips flees in terror.

"I don't know where she is," *I reply, and I marvel that my voice isn't trembling. I don't even have time or the mental capacity to process that Louise was out there still alive somewhere.* "The last time I saw her, she was running off to fight you guys."

Mr. Flynn frowns. "I see. That is indeed regretful," he says and then, raises one eyebrow, his gaze suddenly more intense. It is like he can see into my soul."Is there anything else you would like to tell us Mister Diego?"

I shake my head. "I really want to tell you to go fuck yourself, but that would be rude, and I don't want to be rude to you, because that would be bad," I reply, wanting to stop myself and completely unable to.

Mr. Flynn seems to sense my conundrum and waves my concerns away with a lazy flick of the wrist. "I wouldn't worry about it, Mister Diego. You cannot lie to me. I have that effect on people."

"So I can't lie to you?"

"Not even if you wanted to."

"I'm bored. Can I kill him now?" Mr. Bryce asks in the worst stage whisper ever. "I want to squish him like a little bug."

"Isn't it against the rules to kill another vampire?" I plead, not liking how Mr. Sinnel's breath is so damn close against my neck, hot and unbearable, and stinking like freshly devoured roadkill.

"You are an 'accidental' Mister Diego." Mr. Flynn says, as if it's the most obvious thing in the world.

"Nobody wants you," Mr. Bryce agrees. He grins as he makes a fist, the knuckles cracking one by one as that enormous hand clenches shut.

The kitchen door bursts open, and a hooded woman rushes in, leaving the bright glare of sunlight behind. She is covered head to toe, her face deep in the shadows of the enormous fur-lined hood, the same hood that pulls back to reveal—

"Wazzup motherfuckers!" Beatrice says by way of greeting.

It is immediately clear from the looks on the faces of Mr. Flynn and Mr. Bryce that Beatrice is neither expected or welcome.

"Beatrice," Mr Flynn says levelly and with great disapproval. "Just what do you think you're doing here?"

Beatrice holds up a paper bag with the McDonald's logo, and I can instantly smell the eggs and the sausage from the breakfast McGriddle inside.

"I'm bringing my boy here some much-needed food. He had a pretty busy morning you know. Gotta feed him and keep him strong." Beatrice pauses, and still smiling, says, "now as pleasant as it is to see you boys from the old firm, it always makes me nervous in a stabby kind of way. What the fuck are you doing here?"

"Come now, Beatrice, you know exactly why we're here," Mr. Bryce purrs, more dangerous than any predator.

"We were taking out the trash," Mr Bryce rumbles.

"Still alive there, Bobbikins?" Beatrice yells.

"Don't call me that!" I grumble.

"Does this mean that you have taken responsibility for Mister Diego, then?" Mr. Flynn says drily.

"Yup!" Beatrice says with a grin. "He's my bitch now. Claimed him earlier this morning." Beatrice throws the sandwich to me, and I utterly fail to catch it, you know since I'm still too terrified to move and all that. The sandwich collides with the side of my face and falls to the ground.

Mr Bryce's face creases in disappointment. "We still get to kill him though. Mr. Flynn promised."

Beatrice's face turns icy. "Anybody who touches my bitch is going to be eating his own guts for breakfast instead of a tasty fucking Egg McMuffin."

Mr. Flynn rises to his feet, much like an ultra-stern headmaster who has finally had enough of the petulant student, and Mr. Bryce grins expectantly.

"We have rules, Beatrice—"

"And according to rule four seven six, dash three B, subsection H, if a vampire were to claim an accidental within a twelve-hour period following said vampire's survival of sunrise immolation, the accidental becomes her bitch. I'm paraphrasing the last part for emphasis."

Mr Flynn tilts his head and sighs deeply.

"And I suppose Mister Diego has quite conveniently happened to have survived immolation in the sunlight this very morning?"

I raise my freshly healed arm high into the air, the baby soft skin still significantly paler than the rest of me.

"As a matter of fact, yes," I say a little too enthusiastically. "All the yeses."

Mr. Bryce snorts. "Enough talking," he rumbles, "time to die." He turns and runs at me faster than he ever should have been able to, his enormous hand reaching to squish my head, and I know that this is it, this is the moment where my brains are going to be squished out of my exploded skull. Maybe Mr. Sinnel will eat me with those terrible teeth of his, but I won't care, since I'll be dead. So there's an upside.

Mr. Bryce's dead blow stops inches from my face, and if I pee myself a little, that's none of your goddamn business. There is a brief moment where I glimpse the surprised look on Mr. Bryce's face, but then he is sailing through the air as if he has been struck by a Mack Truck. He collides with the bathroom door, ripping it off its hinges and tumbles as he hits the floor and then the wall. A terrified and bloodied Doreen shrieks incoherently against the far wall, traumatized beyond belief.

It takes me a moment to realize that it is Beatrice who has thrown Mr. Bryce. The same Beatrice who has rescued me and is apparently a fucking badass, not to mention a mastermind for making me go out into the sun, knowing full well what would happen. Holy shitballs!

Beatrice reaches into her coat and produces a katana, the sword sliding from its scabbard with a sharp sounding schnict! Mr. Flynn smirks, unimpressed. He raises a hand and gestures dismissively with his finger.

"Stand down, Mister Sinnel. This one is spoken for," he says as he glances toward the bathroom where Mr. Bryce clambers to his feet. "Mister Bryce, we are leaving. We have been outplayed on this occasion, something that we will not forget soon." He says the last words directly to Beatrice, the threat more than implied.

Beatrice raises her hands in mock surrender. "Oh, by the way, Harry wants to see ol' Bobbikins here. You remember Harry right? Harry, your boss, my boss, total asshole. That Harry." She screws her face up in fake concentration and then smiles broadly, ignoring the steely glare of death from Mr. Flynn. "I think maybe I should have led with that and avoided all the random violence. I mean you guys get so butthurt when you don't get your way..."

Mr. Bryce looks me dead in the eye, and his lip curls.

"Mister Bryce!" Mr. Flynn snaps and looks at Mr. Bryce, who freezes, caught in the act of raising an oversized fist at Doreen. "I implore you not to kill that woman."

Mr. Bryce angrily tears his eyes away from mine. "I never get to kill anything anymore," *he sulks.*

"Nevertheless, we are leaving," Mr. Flynn says. He nods curtly to me. "Good day, Mister Diego. For now."

I watch them leave. Two large black umbrellas have been leaning against the wall, and they are claimed by both men before they make their way out into the blazing sunlight that should have killed any ordinary movie vampire. The door swings shut behind them with a tortured creak.

Reality snaps into place—

Beatrice peered into the bathroom at the sobbing Doreen and then looked expectantly at me. "Well? You coming?"

"Is he still behind me? The other one?" I asked. I could no longer feel Mr. Sinnel's hot breath on my neck, but that doesn't mean anything. Not today.

"He's gone," she replied absently. Beatrice looked back to Doreen as I walked away from the open bedroom door as quickly as possible, still not daring to look behind.

"Hey," Beatrice said to Doreen. "I need you to look at me. Can you do that?"

Doreen wiped at her face and red eyes looked up. Her face relaxed, became more rested, at peace, as she gazed at the beautiful blonde woman in front of her.

"Leave her alone," I said, with a quick glance into the seemingly empty bedroom, looking for some sign as to where Mr. Sinnel has vanished to. The bedroom window is too small and too high-- I caught a glimpse of Tanya's dead face, eyes still open, bloodied and broken, surprised at the turn of events. What was freaky as shit was how Doreen seemed to have forgotten about her dead lover only a few feet away.

"You're pretty," Doreen murmured to Beatrice.

"I hope that means we can be friends," Beatrice said, and Doreen eagerly nodded. "Good, then I'm going to need you to take care of this body and clean yourself up. Can you do that for me?" Doreen nodded again.

"Anything you need," Doreen said with a smile. Her tears have dried, all emotion forgotten as she glanced down at Tanya, suddenly all business. She smiled coyly at Beatrice, blushing red. "Will I get to see you later? I'd really like that." Doreen said.

"Oh I'll find you; don't you worry about that."

"What did you do to her?" I asked Beatrice.

"Glammered the fuck out of her," Beatrice replied and winked at Doreen, who just blushed and continued to cleanup her lover's dead body. "Much better than what old Flynn did to her, if I say so myself, and believe me, I do say so myself. She will do anything I want now, and it's because she thinks she wants to."

My brain was still catching up to everything that had happened in the last ten minutes and was in fact still happening. The presence that the Gentlemen had left in the room made everything feel so empty and lifeless, it felt like my ears should be popping from the change in atmosphere. The one thing that was clear, and very real, was how much Beatrice had just saved my fucking life. And to think I had almost written her off as some crazy drunk.

"Did I mention before that you were a badass?" I asked her.

Beatrice grinned as if it was bloody obvious. She pulled the gigantic hood up on her coat, ready to take a walk in the sunlight.

"Come along Bobby. It's time to meet the vampire king."

Pro-tip for Vampires #8:
You don't have to live your life in the shadows, if you have enough money.

Chapter 19
<u>ALL HAIL THE DRUNKEN KING</u>

There was something almost comforting about riding in the trunk of Beatrice's Dodge Charger, the predatory rumble of the souped-up engine filling the world for a while. The trunk was surprisingly spacious and still had that new car smell, as if Beatrice had driven it right off the showroom floor. If I ever had to recommend a trunk in which to travel or carry a dead body, this one was getting a very high score. The comforter I'd dragged off my bed to protect me from the sun had ended up being a very handy pillow and allowed me to get relatively comfortable.

The only downside to being alone in the darkness, waiting for the ride to end, was that it turned out all I had to occupy myself was my own thoughts, as Beatrice had insisted on taking my phone. For some reason she thought I'd do something stupid like call in the Royal Mounties for a quick rescue or something equally suicidal, like maybe look up how to escape from vampires on the internet, which is exactly reliable as it sounds.

My thoughts were scary and dark, as every single bit of anxiety was taking a tour of my head—a conga line of despair, memory and trepidation. This was mostly thanks to those... *Gentlemen*, who still made the hair stand up on the back of my neck and made my body want to curl up in the fetal position to escape just the *thought* of them. Those *Gentlemen* who had mojoed Doreen into killing the ever loving fuck out of the love of her life, blow by terrible blow shattering bone, splitting flesh and spraying blood, *and still unable to stop--*

Being in the same room as those *Gentlemen* meant you were about to *die, and there was nothing you could do about it, goddammit.* I could still see the blood all over Doreen's face and hear the screams and how she sobbed and cried, but more than anything, the unrelenting *thump... thump... thump...* of her fists beating Tanya to death, but only if I let my mind relax too much.

On the bright side, Beatrice was taking me to see the vampire king who was the boss of the Gentlemen, so that would make him at least twice as horrible. Stomach acid surged into my throat every time I started to think about it. I'd try to think of something else and end up seeing myself turn around face to teeth with Mr. Sinnel... a thought I would rather avoid, *thank you very much.* Which led me back to Tanya's terrible death... you see where this is going, right?

When Beatrice popped the trunk of her car to exhume me, I had just about finally gotten into a somewhat comfortable position or at least one where I didn't feel like my neck was breaking. She peered in at me, framed like a shot in a Tarantino movie with the backdrop of a grey concrete of an underground parking garage. A smile played about her lips in slight amusement.

"Sorry about having to put you in the trunk," Beatrice said by way of greeting.

"It's okay," I reassured her, "between this or burning in the sun, I'll take the trunk any day." I reached to grab inside of the trunk-door. "And you know what, I've been thinking that you don't actually need me--"

"You're scared of meeting Harry."

"Well, he is the vampire king and all that. It could get awkward."

"He's not actually a king. I just call him that to get on his nerves."

"But he's still the big bad boss vampire dude, so hard pass?"

"Oh for fucksake--" Beatrice lunged at me, clearly out of patience and then pulled herself back, curling her hand into a restrained fist. She clenched her teeth and took a deep breath as if to calm herself.

I considered my options, and they weren't looking good. "You're going to drag me out of this trunk are you?"

"That... *is* one of the lesser options I was considering," Beatrice admitted. "Slightly less murdery, but yeah, that *could* work."

The hint was not very subtle, but I got it and decided I had pushed my luck as far as I could with a woman who carried a fucking sword in her coat. Sometimes you gotta know when to quit while you still have a head.

"As enticing as that sounds, I'm going to accept your invitation to meet the vampire king and his merry cohort of maniacal murderers," I replied as I climbed out of the trunk, trying to look as suave as possible. If you've ever had to climb out of the trunk of a car, you know how impossible this is. The last thing I wanted was to trip over my feet and make an ass of myself in front of Beatrice. You could say that I had developed a bit of a crush on her, the same way you could say that the sky is blue, or that sharks like to bite. The worst thing was that even though she scared the shit out of me, *I still wanted to impress her*, so what the actual fuck, right?

The parking garage was huge as parking garages go, and as a space for storing cars, it was futuristic and overly designed. The floor seemed to be made up of black metal grates, the walls lined with strips of dark-grey metal and some kind of high-tech black glass that went up to the thirty-foot ceilings. Considering the quality of cars parked in the oversized spaces, the over-design was quite fitting. The cars slotted into spaces in perfect intervals were all polished black specimens—mostly Ferraris, Lambos, Porsches, and some that I had never seen before but looked like how "fucking expensive" would look if it was a brand. There was not a Lexus or Audi among them, god forbid a Honda or a Ford. As a result, Beatrice's grey Dodge Charger was like a bare-knuckle street fighter facing down Bruce Lee: outclassed no matter how tough it wanted to look. The garage had been designed specifically to send a message to anyone who didn't belong, and to those who did, welcome home.

Beatrice didn't give a shit about any of this, but then again, in her white suit and huge fur coat, she looked right at home. She waggled my cellphone in one hand. "You need to tell your buddy Claude not to be so goddamn clingy. He's texting like a mother whose kid is out past curfew. You'd think you've been abducted by a tall beautiful blonde vampire or something."

"Is this the point where I point out that that's *exactly* what happened, or just focus on the tall and beautiful part?"

Beatrice laughed, a hearty guffaw that came from way down deep, and when she grinned, I could tell that something had changed between us, as if she had just decided that we were going to be friends after all.

"I can see why Louise likes you," she said and passed the phone into my hands. "Text your friend, and tell him to chill."

She walked towards the elevators as if expecting me to follow, so of course I did.

I glanced at the phone, and there was a moment of genuine confusion. "There's only two calls and a text asking me if I wanted sushi or a burrito."

Beatrice stuck her tongue out and squinched her face in disgust. She shook her head and shrugged helplessly. "I know, right? So clingy. Just let him know you're not dead, and let's get this over with."

I fired off a text to Claude: *I'm with Beatrice. Don't freak. Everything is okay. Mostly.*

I thought about the wreck that my place had become and flashed on Tanya's dead face again. I shrugged it off and typed again.

Me: BTW *you might not want to go back to my apartment. Fill you in later, promise.*

I stepped into the elevator behind Beatrice and pocketed the phone. The gleaming brushed-steel doors slid shut, and a black glass panel to the side of the door lit up with the number 44 and an UP arrow. The elevator thrummed like some futuristic device and smoothly shot us upward.

"Remember when I told the Gentlemen that Harry wanted to see you?" Beatrice asked.

I glanced sharply at her, but she was watching the numbers over the door as we ascended, and her expression told me nothing. Yet, there was that feeling of doom that I knew would eventually be followed by an 'oh shit' moment.

"You were lying weren't you?" I asked, impressed with how calm I sounded.

"Yep!"

"Well fuck me running," I sighed. Yeah: this was my life now.

"So with that in mind, I'm going to have a talk with Harry about you," Beatrice said. "He's got this thing about accidentals like you, but I promised Louise I'd take care of you, so I'm gonna see what we can work out. Harry likes me most of the time—" Beatrice considered that for a moment. "Okay, so he mostly tolerates me— wait, you know what? That's a lie. He hates my guts, but I hate him just as much because 'reasons', so this should be a walk in the park!"

I stared at Beatrice, aware that my chances of getting out of this building in one piece had suddenly dropped to zero. Maybe less.

"You couldn't have told me this before we got in the elevator?"

"Yeah, but then you wouldn't have come!" Beatrice beamed happily as if it was the most obvious thing in the world and bopped me on the nose with a finger.

Bing! We had reached floor 44, our apparent destination, and the elevator doors slid open, revealing the slickest office I have ever seen outside of a magazine photoshoot. As if I had expected less after the garage had assured me I was way out of my league just for existing.

I followed Beatrice, my pulse pounding in my ears, as I imagined all the possible ways I was about to be murdered. Beatrice barrelled ahead toward the reception desk at the end of a short corridor. The wall behind the desk was dominated by gigantic aluminum letters that spelled out *The de Biers Company*, with two opaque glass doors in the wall on either side of the sign.

The hallways were paneled in a shiny brown wood-grain, accented by steel or aluminum fluting, with the baseboards and the ceilings lit with hidden strips of warm LED lights that made the black granite floors feel slightly more welcoming. It was classic but modern and futuristic at the same time, if you know what I mean.

Overall it was very impressive and looked extremely legit. It *looked* like a perfectly ordinary office, a point that was made perfectly clear when two women in grey suits, exited what appeared to be a boardroom and walked toward me, deep in conversation.

"—just get me the figures for this quarter and we can push this deal through," the slightly older woman said, fully-immersed in corporate-speak. The women's blue vampire eyes flicked toward me, presumably to make sure I wasn't anybody important, and then looked away once that was confirmed.

At least they weren't there to kill me.

I hurried over to the receptionist's desk and realized that Beatrice had placed her sheathed sword on the desktop. I tried to not look too out of place, like I had every right to be there, but was suddenly conscious of every wrinkle in my new Armani jacket. At least I'd changed my jeans, but the red Hawaiian shirt with the skulls instead of flowers might have been a poor choice. Don't want to give anyone any ideas about my particular skill. The jacket hid it pretty well, but the office was designed to make you aware you were a world of gargantuan deals and extravagant suits.

"—just need five minutes of his time, Pam, and I'm gone," Beatrice informed the receptionist as I caught up to her.

"I should be calling security," Pam whispered, glancing at me. She was a pretty dark-skinned black girl in her late-twenties, tall, model-type features with a mane of deadlocks. Surprisingly, she lacked the tell-tale blue vampire eyes. I wondered if she knew that she worked for vampires, then remembered what Mr.

Flynn and Beatrice had done to control Doreen and realized that it didn't matter. Even if this girl knew the deepest, darkest secrets of vampires, she would never expose them.

"Go ahead," Beatrice said, a slightly dangerous smile playing across her lips, "make the call to security. I haven't had my daily quota of violence yet today. Should be fun."

"Are you actually *threatening* me?" Pam asked, anger flashing in her eyes.

Beatrice smiled charmingly. "Oh don't be ridiculous, Pammy, I'd never threaten *you*. I'm threatening your *security guys*. There's a huge difference."

There was a moment where it felt like the air was going to explode, and all it needed was a flame. Beatrice and Pam stared at each other with "pleasant" smiles on their faces, neither wanting to back down, both silently daring the other to make the next move and goddammit, make it a good one.

I cleared my throat, not sure what to say and leaned close to Beatrice. "Why don't you just do the thing with your eyes? The glammer thing."

That seemed to break the tension.

Pam shifted her gaze to me, smiling sweetly.

"Oh, that doesn't work on me," she said matter-of-factly. "I can't be *glammered*."

Beatrice rolled her eyes and twisted her mouth in consternation. "There's a very small percentage of humans who are immune to any kind mental manipulation. One guess which type Harry just *had* to hire to be his receptionist."

"*Executive* assistant," Pam corrected tersely and proudly. She appraised me and nodded thoughtfully. "You're new..." she said. "Is Beatrice going through all of this trouble for you?"

I shrugged. "I guess so?" I said cautiously, trying very hard not to let Beatrice's baleful stare of total annihilation influence me. "Why does it matter?"

"Oh, she never does anything without a reason. Whatever you've got on her has *got* to be good." Pam considered and picked up the phone. "I can give you five minutes," she said to

Beatrice, "but I'm only doing it because he's kinda cute, not for you."

Beatrice stuck out her tongue, and Pam casually flipped her off with her free hand. I decided in that instant that it might be safer in the boss's office than here, so close to the war between these two women.

"Oh look: a window," I said lamely and turned toward the waiting room to the left of Pam's desk. It was an extension of the reception area, carrying on the high ceilings, but it was the area that actually offered seating on beautiful leather couches and an expansive view of the Toronto city skyline through the big bloody floor-to-ceiling picture window... that had the afternoon sun blasting directly into the room.

Fuck.

I froze. Who the hell would install a window that big in a room where vampires worked? I remembered very clearly—the blast of light and heat— and clenched my teeth expecting the tingle to start any second... but there was nothing.

"What the *fuck*?" I said, slowly raising my hand to the light.

Beatrice appeared next to me after a moment. "That's the culmination of over one-hundred and forty years of funneling money into scientific advances to benefit vampires. Harry saw the big picture before anyone else, you know. He saw the shape of the world that could be, and he made sure we'd be right there, at the top of the world, calling the shots. He developed this glass about ten years ago, and it's installed in more than half the buildings across Toronto, to give us some measure of security and mobility Vampires can walk in the sun again."

A pamphlet was slapped onto my chest, and I looked at it in confusion. It was a de Biers Company pamphlet, open to the 'About Us' page.

"Were you just *reading from a pamphlet*?" I accused.

"Well, most of it is accurate, but Harry does like to blow his own horn," Beatrice said sardonically. She made her way over to the window and tapped on it with her fingernail almost as if she was daring it to break. "The man's a visionary, I'll give that to him. We vampires have it pretty good here in Toronto, especially when you're old enough to remember how things used to be back in the old days, but he can be such a stickler for rules."

I honestly had no idea what to say. "I am so out of my depth right now it's not funny," I admitted, not realizing what I was going to say until I was saying it.

Beatrice wrapped a friendly arm around my shoulder. "Is it too much? Too fast?"

"Little bit," I admitted. "Teeny tiny little bit too much. Maybe I should go? Can I do that? Just leave? Harry doesn't *need* to actually see me does he?"

"Harry will see you now," Pam said from behind me, and Beatrice grinned.

"Suck it up, Daisy, it's showtime!" Beatrice whispered and then brushed past me. I had never felt so alone as I did in that moment.

Beatrice vanished inside the room behind Pam, and I waited, anxious as shit, sure that nothing good was going to come of this situation. The Gentlemen had been bad, but this was the guy they fucking worked for, so he had to be so much worse, right?

I was about to turn towards the window and check out the view from the 44th story over the city, when the door that Beatrice had vanished into opened. Two men exited with Beatrice in tow speaking quickly and intently to the older gentleman. It took me about three seconds to recognize the Middle Eastern man with the intense blue eyes and to finally make the connection with the name.

Harry. Harry de fucking Biers. Claude had mentioned the name after I had been kicked out of that stupid club a couple of days ago, but never in my wildest imagination did I ever think that Harry de Biers III was the de facto king of Toronto vampires. The same guy who had told me to get out of the club--

Holy shit! He had *glammered* me!

The other man was younger, and I couldn't see his face just yet, but there was something about him that was almost recognizable...

Beatrice glanced at me and there was something in her eyes that hadn't been there before, a coldness and caution that made my blood run cold. She forced a smile and nodded before looking away, but I knew what I had seen.

The other man turned and my entire world stopped.

Harry had been a surprise, completely unexpected, but this fuckhead in front of me by the name of Sebastien was something completely different. My body flooded with adrenaline, and I was aware that I had triggered my fangs, even as I lunged at the man in front of me, intending to murder the fuck out of him if it was the last thing I did.

There was a flurry of movement, and a hand clamped down on my speeding fist. I was flipped into the air before I even knew what was happening, landing hard on my back. The wind was forcefully knocked out of me so hard that it was as if I had forgotten how to breathe. That was the least of my problems. Beatrice twisted me over onto my side, pulling my arm back and pushed my face into the carpet, her knee solidly planted on my neck.

"Move again and I'll snap your neck," Beatrice said coldly, and you know what? I honestly believed that she would.

"I'm cool! I'm cool!" I managed to squeak, my lungs finally remembering how to work. Beatrice eased up a little, but only a little.

A shadow fell across me, and for a moment all I saw of Harry was a flawless pair of leather shoes that was probably worth a year of my porn-shop salary. What the hell was it with the shoes today anyway? I tried to look up, but could only move my eyes.

"Let him up," Harry said simply.

Beatrice didn't waste any time. She smoothly yanked me to my feet, making sure to hold onto my arm and twist it behind my back. Unless I cut off my arm at the shoulder, I wasn't going anywhere. And just like that, I was face-to-face with Harry. A terrified and pissed off Sebastien lurked over his shoulder, making sure to stay out of kicking distance.

Harry looked me deep in the eye and nodded, satisfied, then turned his gaze to Beatrice.

"Are you going to be able to stop him from trying to kill my protege?" Harry asked drily.

"He'll do what is required," Beatrice said tersely and I nodded eagerly. Harry's attention was calculating and lacked any warmth. I had never felt so measured and discarded before, so *worthless* and wanted it to stop.

"We'll see," Harry sniffed. He turned and walked away, leaving a stunned-looking Sebatien still glaring at me. Harry called back over his shoulder. "You have seven days to make him presentable Beatrice. If he lives that long."

Sebastien glared at me, biting his lip as if he had something to say, then with a glance at Beatrice, he turned to follow Harry. Only then did Beatrice release her hold on me, shoving me away a little rougher than was strictly necessary.

"Fuck!" Beatrice spat and stomped over to the window, barely holding in her anger.

"Walk away, very, very slowly," Pam whispered from my shoulder. I decided to listen to her and backed away into the reception area, keeping Beatrice within sight at all times. Only when I was by Pam's desk was I able to breathe a little easier. Harry and Sebastien were already gone. Pam shoved a handful of pamphlets at me, and I took them, glad for the distraction.

"What's all this?"

"A little bit of homework for you. History of vampires in Toronto and how the de Biers Company 'is looking to change the image of vampires everywhere.' Think of it as a welcome package." Pam smiled and leaned close. "My gift to you. The look on Sebastien's face just now was spectacular. Damn trust fund babies think they're so goddamn special. It's the training you see. Ten years can do a number on anybody."

"Ten years? For what?"

"To train to become a vampire," Pam said smugly. "It's why accidentals piss off Harry so much. That asshole you almost killed? He's set to be initiated in seven days. Killing him would have flushed away ten years of Harry's investment."

"Ten years? Of what?"

"They train for ten years before they're allowed to be vampires. And you almost killed Harry's protegé. No wonder Beatrice is so pissed off at you."

I had no idea what to say to that. All of this information was making my eye twitch.

One of the brochures caught my eye. "'*A Guide to Accumulating Wealth after Death*', '*So I'm a Vampire... Now What?*'" I read aloud, and looked at Pam, feeling more than a slight panic as my heart rate increased. "Is this for real?"

There was a crash from the other room as Beatrice threw something. She roared, and I flinched, suspecting with about 100% accuracy that I was the reason for her tantrum.

"Initiation is in a week at HTDK," Pam said, making her way back behind her desk. "Beatrice is sticking her neck out for you, so don't fuck it up." She shifted her attention and focus, effectively turning me off. The phone rang. "The de Biers Company, Harry's office. How can I help?"

Another crash as Beatrice threw something else.

I wondered if vampires could become invisible. It would've been a handy skill at the moment.

***

The elevator ride down to the garage was spent in uncomfortable silence. Bonus points for not getting murdered by Beatrice, right? When the silence became unbearable, I finally spoke up. "What the fuck just happened up there?"

Beatrice spoke from between clenched teeth. "I can't train you," she said with what seemed like great effort.

That was totally not what I was expecting and I told her so in the most eloquent way that I knew would sway her opinion: "*Why the fuck not? You promised Louise!*"

Yeah... not the wisest thing to do. Beatrice punched me the fuck out.

Pro-tip for Vampires #29:
True love still sucks.

Chapter 20
THE NEMESIS AND THE LADY

When I came to, my head screaming as if icepicks were being repeatedly stabbed into the top of my skull, pressure pushing against my temples in a way that indicated my head was about to explode, the air reeked of rubbing alcohol, bad news, and despair. I didn't want to open my eyes, but the pain gave me no choice in the matter, because pain takes no prisoners and I was its bitch. My eyes popped open and proved my worst fears to be true as the light sent sharp spears of pain into my eyeballs, but at least that allowed me to see that I was laying on a bed in the Emergency Room. Sure enough, there was Dr. Mendelssohn sitting at the side of the bed tapping on an iPad in her lap, apparently not at all concerned with her patient, namely, me. I was about to inform the doctor of this obvious lapse in her duty, when a horrible thought bounced into my aching skull and tossed my self-pity into the gutter where it belonged.

Jaime.

Jaime was dating the lead henchmen for an evil vampire syndicate.

What if Sebastien planned to drain Jaime on his first day as a vampire? Or sell her to a weird vampire cult as a "donor?" There must be weird vampire cults. Right?

"I have to warn Jaime about Sebastien," I said, or at least *tried* to say. My jaw audibly clicked into place, and I almost mangled my tongue. "Oh fuck me!" I sputtered, hands going to my mouth. How much more pain was in store for me anyway?

"I'd slow down if I were you," Dr. Mendelsohnn said, eyes glued to her iPad as if she was watching porn. Doctor porn. "Beatrice punched you pretty hard. Broke your jaw in three places. Since she's the one who brought you here, I'm going to guess that she may have a soft spot for you. Or she wants to get you healed up so she can do it again. You never know with Beatrice."

"Why does it hurt so much?" I groaned, trying to focus through the pounding in my head. There was rising pressure, almost unbearable, causing me to gasp, which in turn caused my jaw to click again-- and then, just like that, the pain was gone. Poof. It was as if someone had flipped a switch. "Woah."

Dr. Mendlesohnn rolled her chair over to my side with a practised move and began to examine me, starting with my eyes and holding me firm with a glare when I flinched.

"Oh, that's just from getting punched. Not quite like it is in the movies, you know. If you get hit hard enough to get knocked out, it's more likely than not that you've suffered a mild concussion. Get knocked out enough times, and you can end up in a vegetative state. The brain doesn't like being jerked around you know. Just be glad that you're a vampire, and you actually heal from such injuries, so you get to indulge a little. Yay." Dr. Mendelsohnn paused. "Pro-tip, since you're new to all of this: don't go around punching humans. You could literally kill someone."

I flashed on the terror on Sebastien's face as I had lunged at him and shifted uncomfortably. That douchebag was still human, and I had almost killed him, and for what? *For dating Jaime?* That was a douchebag move if ever there was one, even if the motherfucker deserved it.

Remember that whole thing about me not remembering that Sebastien had murdered me? Yeah, it was back again to fuck with me once again. While I didn't actively remember it, some part of me did and it was trying to tell me in the only way it could. My instincts were trying to take over and offer clues. For me, it was a flash of *blood... and Sebastien looking down on me...* and this undefinable *rage.* It was the same rage that I had felt when I had lunged at him in Harry's office. Every instinct I had was screaming at me to *murder* Sebastien, screaming that he was dangerous. *What the actual fuck?*

I shook it off, not liking these dark thoughts.

"Good to know. About the punching thing," I said. "How long was I out for?"

"About four hours. Your regenerative-ability is quite impressive. This kind of injury usually takes a good eight hours of recovery."

"Should have seen me this morning," I tried to quip.

"I really don't want to know."

"But the—"

"Not another word, Mister Diego," Dr. Mendelsohnn said, "and let's try not to make this a regular thing, okay? You're making me do actual work for a change." She turned to leave, her hand sliding into her pocket and she paused, then produced a folded-over piece of paper. "Oh I almost forgot. Beatrice left this for you."

I took the note.

"Sorry I killed you," I read.

She had even drawn a smiley face.

***

"You've got to be kidding me," I said staring at the digital billboard outside the main doors of the hospital. It was one of the modern ones that could display video and cycled through a series of advertisements, one of which happened to be for the de Biers Company. In a case of the universe seriously fucking with me, the model with the lustrous hair chosen to be the face of the de Biers Company was, of course, Sebastien. *Fuck my life, right?*

I had to stand on the sidewalk next to Sebastien's smug face for the longest three minutes of my life before my Uber finally showed up. I flipped the bird to the advertisement as I made my way to the car.

The Uber driver was a no-nonsense Chinese guy in his early twenties. He had a moustache that was more mouth than actual stache, the thin wisps of hair on his upper lip making a valiant but doomed effort as they struggled against genetics. Speaking of facial hair, I rubbed my recently-healed jaw. I hadn't shaved in days, and my suave scruff had thickened into an itchy but very determined beginnings of a beard. As the car pulled away from the hospital, I contemplated texting Jaime, but there were a couple of problems with that. A) Jaime had blocked my number and B), I didn't know exactly what I should say to her about Sebastien that didn't make me look like a jealous ex-boyfriend stalker. *Fuck.* I texted Claude instead.

Me: *Hey dude, where are you?*

There was a moment and then the three dots of eternal typing appeared before a message popped up.

Claude: *NYC. Business meeting for this new gig. Back tomorrow.*

Me: *I suddenly feel abandoned.*

Claude: *You're the one who went gallivanting with Beatrice. How did that turn out? Useful I hope.*

Me: *Can you skip it? Official best friend business here. I need you man.*

Claude: *Tell me tomorrow. In the middle of something here. Fucking Russians just showed up.*

Me: *Seriously??????*

There was a pause, and then a red exclamation popped up under my last text: *Message Not Delivered. Resend?* I tried again and waited for a second. The message popped up again.

"Fuck!" I swore. I'd wanted to tell him that I had discovered Sebastien was going to be a vampire in a week, and now that was on hold. This is why you don't bury the lede: if you have something important to say, then just say it upfront. I needed

Claude to talk me down from going to talk to Jaime or at least plan how to approach it without ending up with something heavy and/or sharp being thrown at my recently-healed, scruffy face. Claude's job was to stop me from doing anything idiotic, and I had a feeling I was about to do something idiotic, but in my defence, it was better than not doing anything at all, right?

"Hey," I said to the driver, and he glanced back at me, "I need to change the destination, okay?"

"Just do it in the app, man," the driver said. "It's right there. See it?"

"Yeah, I know, dude just letting you know," I grumbled as I typed in the new address..

My phone binged as a message arrived. I glanced at the notification. There was a cluster of bings as more messages arrived one after the other. *Bing! Bing! Bing!*

Sammy: *Where the fuck are you?*

Sammy: *Get your ass to the store right fucking now.*

Sammy: *Jaime is here to murder you.*

Sammy: *bring donuts.*

✳✳✳

Sometime in the eighteen minutes it took to drive from the hospital to the Porn Emporium, the snow had started again. It was the wet hard-hitting snow that felt more like the sky was spitting than anything else, and wasn't sticking to the ground long enough to accumulate, but instead simply made everything miserable. I'd started feeling like a hero on a mission to save the girl from a douchebag, so the weather was adding to the sense of drama of the night, especially with the way the lights of the buildings reflected off the wet asphalt. Any wetter and it would have been the wrong kind of movie altogether, with dudes fighting in the rain and being all angsty, and I wasn't ready for that level of drama.

A blast of wind struck me as I exited the Uber, whipping my coat behind me dramatically, as I walked toward the door; I can honestly say that I felt like a bonafide badass.

When I opened the door to the Porn Emporium, I expected the moment to last forever, Jaime turning to look, our eyes meeting from across the room, the lights dimming dramatically so it seemed that we were the only people in the world... but I'm gonna shit all over that romantic notion with a dose of reality. All that happened was that she turned... and there was nothing at all, just the realization from the look on her face that that motherfucker Sebastien had gotten to Jaime first and she was out for blood. This wasn't a rescue: it was an ambush.

I approached Jaime, while Sammy watched from behind the counter reaching down to produce a small red-and-white striped-box of "movie popcorn," and I resisted the urge to flip her off. I kept my focus on Jaime.

I had fantasized many times over the past six months about coming face-to-face with Jaime again, and in all of those scenarios, never once had I imagined that it would happen in aisles two and six of the Porn Emporium. My fantasies were more chick flick-inspired—a park with swans floating in a pond or a candlelit restaurant. Not once did I imagine we'd be surrounded by dildoes, pocket-pussies, and GILF porn. I really should have picked a better aisle to stop at than aisle six where the DVD cover of a granny in the middle of a circle of cocks wasn't staring a challenge at the camera. This was not how reunion fantasies were supposed to go.

"How did you find out I've been seeing Sebastien?" Jaime asked, quietly and perfectly calmly, and I knew I was sunk. I would have preferred a yelling Jaime to a calm Jaime, because at least that one still had emotions. "Was it Louise? Is that why she's been avoiding my calls?"

"Can we do this somewhere else?" I pleaded. "There's a lot that's happened—"

"You followed him to his office and then assaulted him in front of his boss? What the fuck, Bob?"

Okay, so we were doing this then, right here, right now.

"I didn't follow him!" I replied, my mind racing and jumping to the defence, just to buy time. "I didn't even know he worked there, I swear!"

"You're not even *denying* it!" Jaime glared at me and grabbed the closest projectile, which happened to be a pink light-up dildo.

"Because it's not that simple!" I said, flustered. "It's—"

"Don't you dare say that it's complicated!" Jaime snapped, brandishing the pink dildo.

"— complicated!" I finished lamely. How the fuck had I turned into one of those blithering idiots from the rom-coms? No fair!

Jaime rolled her eyes, and I slumped in defeat.

"You know I'm going to have to throw this now, right?"

"Throw it, I deserve it."

Jaime aimed and tossed it overhand. The pink dildo bounced off the side of my head with a dull thud, then bounced into the aisle six in a whirl of blinking LEDs encased in pink rubber. Jaime snickered, and I glanced at her hopefully.

"Your aim sucks," I noted with a glance at the dildo, which was busy vibrating its way in an uneven circle as if playing a bizarre game of Spin-the-Dildo.

"But I hit you," Jaime protested.

"Exactly."

"*You* try throwing a dildo," Jaime snickered.

"It's good to see you again, Jaime," I ventured. "I was hoping for less yelling, but it is what it is, right?"

Jaime grimaced and looked away. She rolled her eyes when she noticed Sammy watching us over the container of popcorn, but when Jaime turned back, she was all business, only slightly less pissed off. Also, tired.

"You still haven't answered my question," Jaime said.

"That's the wrong question," I replied. "Sebastien is not a good person. He's definitely not the person you think he is. You know who he works for, right?"

"Uh, huh." Jaime obviously wasn't buying it. I could tell she had already made up her mind, but I still had to try, right? She continued. "I'm going to humour you Bob. Tell me exactly what makes my new *boyfriend* not a good person, other than the fact that he's not you?"

I opened my mouth to tell her the truth, that Sebastien worked for the vampire king of Toronto and that he was about be turned into a vampire in a week... then I realized just how *fucking stupid* that was going to sound. See? This is why I needed Claude to tell me that talking Jaime about Sebastien was a bad idea.

"I... I can't do that," I mumbled, then tried to recover, "but you gotta trust me on this—"

"Is he *cheating* on me?"

"No, but—"

"Is he stealing from me?"

"No."

"Is he a fucking *addict* who's putting my life at risk by hiding drugs from his dealer in the fucking apartment?"

Ouch. That one hurt. "Jaime—"

"Bob, you don't get to judge *anybody*. Sebastien could be beating my ass bloody on a nightly basis, and I'd still trust him over you. What happens in my life is none of your fucking business. You gave that up."

That was my big "aha" moment right there where I finally got it about how those guys or girls in the chick-flicks always seemed caught off guard and literally couldn't find the right thing to say. Granted, the writers always did a shitty job (sorry writers) because all the characters had to do was blurt out the truth, and there would be no misunderstanding at all, and everything would be resolved twenty minutes before the big dramatic airport chase scene. I was *living* the moment where I could literally say nothing to salvage the situation because anything I had to say made me look like a jealous ex.

Your boyfriend is going to be a vampire!

How do you know that?

Because I'm a vampire.

Fuck you Bob. Fuck you very much.

See what I'm working with here? All I could do was stand there and say nothing, and relive the shame of what I had done to Jaime. All of it was true, so what the hell did I have to say?

Jaime strode towards the exit, and I stepped aside, unable to look her in the eye. She stopped when she got next to me, so of course, I looked up, hesitant. Her eyes brimmed with tears, and all I wanted to do was reach out and brush them away.

"Give me a reason not to hate you, Bob," she whispered. "Tell me something true."

"I don't ever want to do anything to hurt you," I said, meaning every word of it but knowing that it just wasn't good enough.

"And yet, here we are," Jaime sighed. She reached out and stroked my cheek, the way she always used to ... then her eyes widened as she really got a good look at my eyes for the first time. "Holy shitballs! What the fuck did you do to your eyes?"

I hesitated, wondering what she was even talking about, actually forgetting that my eyes had changed colour--

"Contact lenses," I lied. "Thought they'd make me look cool."

Jaime opened her mouth to speak, then tightened her lips. The sudden temptation came to try to glammer her just like Beatrice had done to Doreen, but even though my mouth opened to say the words, I hesitated, and then... changed my mind. It just felt so *wrong* to do that to her. *What the fuck was I even thinking?* Plus, I didn't exactly know *how* to do it, so there was that.

Jaime took her hand away from my face, and my heart dropped a hundred feet.

"Goodbye, Bob," Jaime said, and that was it.

I didn't say anything. I didn't turn to watch her leave. I couldn't. Tears didn't suddenly spring to my eyes, so fuck you for thinking it, and even if it did happen, it's just allergies okay?

Sammy had put the popcorn away and looked a little embarrassed for me. She even shrugged an apology at me. Poor Benjamin made himself busy stocking a shelf, trying hard to appear as if he hadn't been watching.

The door chimed as Jaime exited. A second passed, and the bell chimed as the door opened again. I turned, stupidly hoping that it was Jaime rushing back to tell me that everything was forgiven and how right I was. It's how these situations go in chick-flicks, okay? It's more drama.

But it wasn't Jaime. Not even close. It was the Boss, and he had a smug look on his face, his lip curled with derision, and I could tell he had been planning this moment for a long time. He was probably even going to say something really cliché—

"Well, look what the cat dragged in," the Boss said.

See what I told you? Total cliché.

"Oh, hey, Mister—" I said, or at least started to say before he raised a hand to cut me off.

"Shut your fucking mouth, Bobby. Let me enjoy firing your ass, leaving us in the lurch like you did."

I snapped. I didn't even feel it coming, no building rage or anything, just sudden blinding rage. I walked toward the little man, eyes burning and felt it, that instant *connection*, my mind to his mind, and I knew exactly what to do. I felt the effects of the *glammer*, and I *embraced* it.

"No," I whispered as the Boss froze in his tracks, eyes wide.

"You're right," he whispered. "That's not fair is it?"

"I need this job," I whispered intently, and the Boss nodded in agreement, after all, he was a fair man, a little tough but fair.

"It's good to have you back, Bobby. Still good for the night shift right?"

"You should give me a raise," I pressed and that met with some resistance and bewilderment. He frowned in response and shook his head. Apparently that was going too far.

"Welcome back!" the Boss exclaimed as if this was all his idea. He grabbed me by the arm and dragged me toward Sammy and Benjamin, suddenly ebullient. I noticed the stunned expression on Sammy's face, mouth and eyes wide, staring in disbelief. "Hey, everybody: Bobby's back!"

"No. Fucking. Way." Sammy said once the Boss had disappeared up the stairs. "What the fuck did you do to him? Is it drugs? It's got to be drugs right?" She finally got a good look at my eyes and gasped. "No fucking way those are contact lenses. Bob, for real though: what the fuck happened to your eyes?"

"I gotta go," I mumbled and turned away, painfully aware of how my eyes looked. Even my tongue couldn't stop running over the pointed nubs of my incisors that were retracted for the moment, reminding me that I was a vampire. There was a stab of guilt at glammering the Boss like that, but he had caught me at the wrong moment, and he had been someone to lash out at—

I grabbed a pair of cheap sunglasses from the rack on the counter and stumbled out of the store. How had everything had gotten so fucked up? I was supposed to be the hero, goddamit.

Pro-tip for Vampires #22:
If you don't have the rulebook, you don't
know which rules you can break.

Chapter 21
GUYS LIKE ME

The bus pulled up to the stop as I exited the Porn Emporium, and I only hesitated for a second before my instincts kicked in and I ran for the corner as if all of Pavlov's dogs were chasing after me. It didn't even occur to me that I was wearing the better part of a suit that should never be forced to endure public transit. I covered the fifty-feet faster than I had expected and jumped into the front doors behind a way too-cocky Millenial in his cheap jacket and vintage Misfits t-shirt. I was operating mostly on automatic and by the time the bus pulled away from the curb, easing its way into traffic, I realized that I had actually meant to call an Uber. I settled into the rhythm of the bus easily enough, until I caught sight of one of the ads above the windows.

Sebastian leered at me from the de Biers Company poster, mocking me with his perfect looks and stupid fucking hair, until I had to turn away and look somewhere else. Yet the emotions burned deep inside; Jaime's stinging rejection was something I had to deal with. I couldn't save her from Sebastien. She had made her choice, and anything I did would end in disaster. And in seven days, that motherfucker was going to be a vampire.

A vampire just like me. Well, not exactly like me. He had his goddamned fortune. Probably a castle too. Maybe even a cape somewhere with a high collar and everything.

I rocked back and forth with the rhythm of the ride, hiding behind my sunglasses, wanting nothing more than to pretend I was still human. Riding the bus among the normal people making their way home, was as normal and as human as it could get.

"Bobby, is that you?" a familiar voice said, and I turned to see Crazy Mary making her way from the back of the bus, a big shit-eating grin on her face. "Didn't recognize you."

The bus veered to a stop, and I stumbled, my face colliding with the metal pole. The cheap sunglasses were knocked off my face, but I grabbed them before they could fall, my reflexes kicking in. I grinned at that small triumph, a grin that slowly faded as I saw the way Crazy Mary looked at me.

Terror. Sheer unmitigated terror twisted her face.

"You ain't no Bobby!" She hissed at me and spat on the ground. "You got them eyes, you soulless freak. I know what you are!"

"Mary—' I tried to calm her down, and she pulled away as if my touch was poison. I was suddenly painfully aware of everybody on the bus staring at me and kept my hands to myself.

"Motherfucking chupacabra!" Crazy Mary shrieked, and shoved through the doors, rushing off the bus to get away from me.

She screamed obscenities at the bus as we pulled away into the night.

I had never felt so alone.

***

Guess whose face was on the side of the covered bus stop when I got off the bus?

Fuck you, universe.

There was a white Tesla Model S parked in front of my apartment complex, a car that stood out as clearly not belonging. All of the other cars parked on both sides of the street were a mixture of early-to-recent models of Nissans, Toyotas, and other ordinary high carbon-emissions vehicles. That Tesla was definitely way too slick-looking for my neighbourhood. You might as well have put up a billboard next to the car saying "drug dealer."

This thought was confirmed a moment later as a Latino man exited from the passenger side, the large fur-lined hood on his oversized winter coat pushed back far enough to expose his face. It was my favourite upstairs neighbour and drug dealer, Julio.

"Hey, Roberto!" Julio called out when he saw me, and he was way too cheerful, he had never been this cheerful, and was I freaking out a little, no I wasn't, I was freaking out a lot!

"Julio," I said with a nod, heart thumping away in my chest like an over-excited chihuahua on crack. What did he know about Doreen and the deceased Tanya? He was going to ask me about them, I could feel it.

"You ain't seen Tanya and Doreen have you?"

"Not since this morning," I said cautiously. "They were having a fight last time I saw them."

"Huh. Well, this ain't like them at all," Julio said thoughtfully, then brightened up. "They told you about my offer right? So you had time to think about it. My business partner's in the car, and he would really love an answer, know what I mean?"

I nodded carefully. What did I have to lose? "Just for the week right?"

"My man! Come on, it's in the trunk," Julio exclaimed, doing what he thought was a decent Denzel Washington impression.

He led the way to the back of the car, and I followed. "Just for ol' time's sake, I'm gonna throw in a little sumthin' extra for you, howzat?"

The trunk to the Tesla popped open, and Julio beckoned me closer, so I did. There was a black duffle bag inside, similar to other bags I had stashed for Julio. I knew the steps to this dance: I was the one who had to pull the drugs out. I stepped forward and reached into the trunk for the bag—

There was a sharp pain in the side on my neck and then a rush of adrenaline that threatened to overwhelm my senses as the familiar heady sensation of heroin streamed through my veins. More pain on the left side of my neck, and I turned to Julio, seeing the pair of syringes in his hands, emptied of their contents. I felt the rush in my veins and the throb, throb, throb of my heart pumping blood and heroin to my head. Julio was speaking, and I really had to focus to understand—

"—fucking son-of-a-bitch, this is what you get when you fuck with me and mine."

I shook my head, everything moving so slow in my mind, the movement taking forever, Julio's words slurring and turning into an unintelligible groan, the flying spittle from his mouth hanging in the air, the droplets of the spray spreading in an ever-expanding mist. A man came around the side of the car, the driver, and he was caught in the slow-motion that existed only in my mind, but even so, I recognized that stupidly-handsome face that really needed punching, and then I was face-to-face with Sebastien.

Clarity came rushing back all at once, sudden sobriety as my body somehow absorbed the drugs that had been injected. I shuddered, shaking it off and realized that I had triggered my fangs again, a surge of good adrenaline burning through my veins.

"You motherfucker!" I snarled.

Sebastien reached into Julio's open jacket and yanked out a pistol from the shoulder holster, pulling a surprised Julio away from me at the same time. The gun came down at me, and I could see him pulling the trigger, and I moved out of the way of where he was pointing. BLAM! And the bullet missed. Sebastien squeezed the trigger again, but I was already moving, like Neo in the Matrix, and did I dodge that bullet? You bet your ass I did. BLAM!

"Stop moving, you fucking fuck!" Sebastien screamed at me.

"You can't shoot me, motherfucker," I slurred through my fangs, trying not to bite my tongue.

Sebastien shrugged in confusion. "What's that? I can't understand you with the fangs."

I pushed up with my tongue, and the fangs retracted. "I said you can't shoot me! I'm a goddamn vampire."

Julio had been watching all of this with a shocked look on his face, and now he staggered back, eyes wide in terror. Of course, he then tripped and fell over his own feet. As if by instinct, his phone had appeared in his hand as if he as catching all of this crazy shit on camera for his YouTube channel.

Sebastien steadied himself. "You should have kept the fangs out," he said and emptied the gun into my chest. I would like to say I dodged every one, but I don't think he even missed once. It was as if my vampire powers switched off when I retracted my fangs, something that Sebastien obviously knew about, and I had fallen for his lame-ass trick like some amateur. No: like some accidental.

BLAM! BLAM! BLAM! BLAM! BLAM! The bullets thudded into and through me before I could even twitch or even register that I had been shot. It was difficult to breathe, and it was all I could do to look down at my chest, now red with blood, ripped fabric in many places from the bullets.

I slumped to my knees, all strength going out of my legs. Sebastien walked over to me, that same cocky expression on his face that he used in all of the fucking ads that had been taunting me all night, and I realized that he wore the exact same type of shoes as Harry. Nice fucking shoes.

"Stay dead this time," Sebastien suggested.

I looked up to tell him to go fuck himself, but I didn't have a chance.

That motherfucker shot me in the face.

End of Season 1

Author's Note

Fucking hell, this is weird.

Weird because I thought that the next time I would be doing this, it would be for the second book in the series. Weird because I had reached the dreaded act 3 of the second book, just past the 100K mark and was feeling pretty good about it. Weird because here I am, once again rewriting this book because of some feedback I got about the flow and structure of SO I MIGHT BE A VAMPIRE.

Truthfully, this was supposed to be the easiest rewrite and clean up. I was supposed to go in, add a few new chapters for the beginning so that we could approach the story more linearly. So You Used to be Human was completely linear, so that set the baseline and the tone, so when I got into So I'm a Vampire... Now What? I followed that same structure. Completely linear. The only one that was told differently was So I Might Be a Vampire.

Which I had polished and edited.

And published.

Awkward, right?

So I Might Be a Vampire was perfect for a Netflix adaptation, as far as I saw it. So when I got a very detailed bit of feedback from Wattpad Stars that they would have to pass on it unless some issues were addressed, I took a moment to swear profusely, had a tantrum as is my right as an author... and then got right to work breaking down the story. The notes were specific to pacing and the broken structure of the timeline and echoed some of the comments readers had left, so I had a choice to be lazy and bitter... or to go in and fix it. It could be restructured, and the problems could be improved. At around this same time, Wattpad had also introduced a new style of novels called "Infinite Stories," which would be an ongoing serialization. I took a look at everything I had written for Bob with all three of the books and knew that it would be a perfect fit. I met had Debra Goelz a little earlier, and we had clicked easily as friends. After reading some chapters I had written, she admitted that she was a professional editor and took a certain measure of joy from reading my stories about Bob. When I told her about my plan for restructuring the series, we partnered up with a rewrite. I naively thought at the time that it would be easy: all I had to do was write to a certain point, and then the rest of the story just needed touching up after that.

How Not to Vampire was born, and we spent the next two months building out the chapters to aim for a June release and be at least ten to fifteen chapters in. The initial plan was 25 chapters at 2500 words apiece, and following our Save the Cat beat sheet that laid out the entire arc of season 1, we had a solid plan.

Then Infinite Stories got scaled back, but you know what? We went ahead anyway. We would produce our own infinite story, seasons and all and see how the readers would react to Bob and friends' new shenanigans.

This is some of the best writing that I've done in years, and I did take joy in writing down Bob's adventures. A lot of it was reliving what I had written before, but now it was with a different depth and perspective that Deb forced me to look at. She pushed the difficult questions, so I got to meet my characters all over again and took joy in reintroducing them to the world. Bob and Claude's relationship is so much more nuanced now. Sammy has depths that should never be looked at too closely. Jaime is three-dimensional and actually has a presence and lines in this version. The Gentlemen are scary as fuck in this version. Louise is an absolute delight, and I can't wait to write more of her. And of course, Beatrice got a brand new intro that was more epic than I could have imagined. She's sprinkled in here and there from chapter two onward, but her real entrance is pure Beatrice in every way.

I'll be honest: I had planned to go all the way to chapter 30 and to end the arc properly, putting us well over 100K words, with a resolution of the Sebastien situation and Bob's introduction to the vampire world, but I realized something once I had rewritten the scene where Bob gets shot in the face: we had an arc, and as a serial, we had the perfect cliffhanger. After looking over the story's arc, I also realized we had ended almost where we had begun: with Bob making a bad decision about drugs. Julio shot him in the original version, but with Sebastien doing the act this time and tricking Bob... it was almost too perfect an ending to pass up.

Anyway, season 2 picks up and heads us into dangerous territory. Some of you who had read So I Might Be a Vampire might think you know what's coming, but there are some huge surprises coming. This story is evolving while staying true to itself.

And yes: I'm never going to stop saying "fuck", so let's just have fun with it.

Oh, and for the last time: no, I am not a vampire

Thanks for joining me on this journey. Deb has kicked my ass into making sure that everything made sense, and she really was the perfect editor. I owe her a massive debt of gratitude... and free artwork for a lifetime!

I owe a lot to the late-night sprinting sessions on the Discord server where a bunch of us would gather throughout the day or night and set a timer to write as much as we could *for thirty minutes or an hour at a time. There was no pressure to produce, although it could get a little competitive; it was just a sense of fun, community, and writing with friends, and that was valuable. None of us were writing alone.*

I'm proud to know such a tremendously talented bunch of writers, so thank you, Wattpad, for bringing us together. Shout out to my fellow Wattpad stars and sprinters Van_Carley, K Edward Stewart, Ava Larksen, Mason Fitzzy, Jordan Lynde and AmiTheDarkLady for keeping me company in the dark hours of the night.

PaulaPDX, AW Frasier, MB Druidrose, Tamara Lush, Erich W, Sabrina Blackburry, Milo Nelakho, Arveliot, Jane Peden, Sam le Fou, Zoe Blessing and all of my fellow Upstarts, thank you for keeping me sane through what has got to be one of the most fucked up years of our lives. You guys are amazing and I'm glad to know so many talented people.

Clarissa North: you are a peach and an inspiration, and I'm glad to have you as a friend.

Also: fuck you, Clarissa. You know what you did.

Rodney V. Smith
September 20, 2020

About the Author

photo by Angela Durante Dukat

Rodney V. Smith has been writing stories from the time he could hold a pencil. Born in Barbados, he has written short stories, screenplays and webseries. He is also a prolific artist in a variety of mediums, including oils and acrylics, and digital art. He once considered a profession as a comic book writer and illustrator, but gave it up when he discovered screenwriting and filmmaking (although he occasionally dabbles).

He is the president and one of the founding members of the Independent Web series Creators of Canada (IWCC) and has written and produced several webseries including the critically acclaimed "Dominion" and the sci-fi adventure "Out of Time" (now on Amazon Prime). He has scripted, filmed and produced over ten short films and independent feature films.

His novel THE CANEFIELD KILLER won the 2018 Wattys Award and was subsequently accepted into Wattpad Paid Stories.

www.ingramcontent.com/pod-product-compliance
Lightning Source LLC
Chambersburg PA
CBHW071525120726
47907CB00013B/1012